and the frozen man

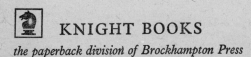

KNIGHT BOOKS

the paperback division of Brockhampton Press

ISBN 0 340 10409 1

This edition first published 1971 by Knight Books,
the paperback division of Brockhampton Press Ltd, Leicester

Printed and bound in Great Britain by
Cox & Wyman Ltd, London, Reading and Fakenham

Text copyright © 1970 Angus MacVicar
Illustrations copyright © 1970 Brockhampton Press Ltd

Contents

Super Nova and the frozen man

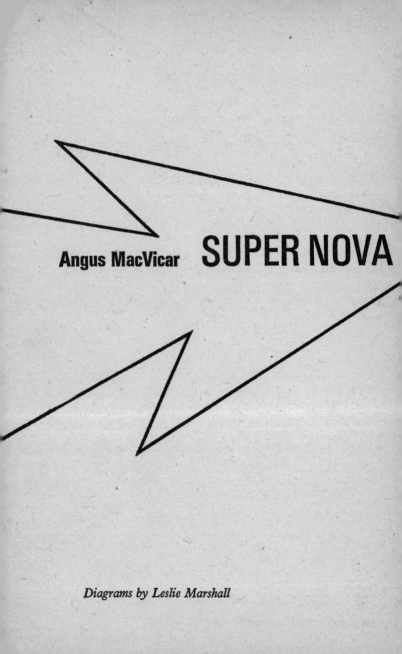

Angus MacVicar   # SUPER NOVA

Diagrams by Leslie Marshall

1 | Mystery in the Martian Sector

THE tiny, ball-shaped reconnaissance ship, in free fall, came speeding in from outer space and entered the charted area surrounding Earth.

Alfredo Togneri, the dark-skinned Italian pilot, looked out at the stars, flicked a computer switch and made a note of the reading. Finally he consulted the flight-plan and grinned across at his German co-pilot.

'We made it, Hermann. Spaceway 69, Martian Sector, right on the nose.'

'Yes. I have observed.'

Hermann Buedeler was a fair young man of few words; but he looked and sounded as pleased as did his commander.

They had every reason to be pleased. This was the end of a reconnaissance flight to Mars, during which they had spent 260 days on the outward journey, 446 days in orbit, probing and photographing, and 250 days on the return flight. In a few hours now *Ariel 7* would dock at Alpha Main. Soon they would see Earth again and begin to enjoy the rewards of more than two and a half years of disciplined, hermit-like existence.

Hermann said: 'A drink to success, Alf?'

'Sure. Splice the mainbrace as they used to say in the English Navy.'

But as Hermann reached for the last bottle of glucose lemon in the store-cupboard the lights flickered. Pointers on the instrument panel did a crazy dance.

Hermann's gloved hand stopped in mid-air. 'What is it?'

'I don't know.' There was tension in Alfredo's voice.

Again the lights flickered. The pointer on the speed indicator leapt across the dial, then settled back to a much higher figure than normal.

Alfredo took another reading from the computer. He frowned and exclaimed: 'We're off course! Heading west-north-west. Jets!' he commanded. 'Auxiliary jets, full!'

Hermann leant sideways, thrust down on the lever. The power indicator in the panel ought to have glowed red. It remained blank.

'Jets negative!' he exclaimed, unnecessarily. His tone had an edge of fear.

Alfredo experienced momentary panic. After their long journey he and Hermann were almost at the end of their physical and mental resources. For a moment the prospect of an imminent return to Earth had raised their morale. Now this emergency, occurring on the very threshold of success, caused them more distress than otherwise it might have done.

But Alfredo's disciplined training soon reasserted itself. Flogging his tired brain into action, he said: 'Probably an electrical fault. Institute system check as per schedule.'

'Okay.' Hermann unbuckled his harness, weaved left for the tool-kit.

Steadily the speed indicator pointer moved up across the dial. As with uncharacteristic urgency Hermann began to uncover the mass of wires behind the instrument panel, Alfredo switched on the radar and directed its beam in the direction they were travelling. After a few seconds a scatter pattern appeared on the screen. He held the scanner steady. There was a faint ping, and he stared incredulously at a pin-head of light in the centre of the pattern.

'Any luck?' he said, his voice cracking on the casual note he had intended.

'Not yet.' Sweat stood out on Hermann's forehead.

For a third time the lights flickered and the pointers danced. With hands which shook slightly Alfredo riffled through the charts. He found the one he wanted, checked *Ariel 7* at B-lat 3,

A-long 94. Using his space-range calculator, he looked for something on the chart in the position indicated by the radar. There was nothing.

He shivered. The bright pin-head was growing in size, the pinging sound in volume. The ship's speed was increasing at a terrifying rate. It had become dauntingly obvious that in less than an hour, if they failed to take avoiding action, *Ariel 7* must collide with a solid body, whatever that body might be.

Hermann had now left the instrument panel and was inspecting a junction in the motor bulkhead.

Suddenly he shouted: 'Got it, Alf! Igniter circuit. Blown fuse.'

'Thank God! Make it quick!'

In less than a minute the jets were burning. Five minutes after that *Ariel 7* regained her course. The radar screen was empty, the instrument panel at rest.

In their exhausted state Alfredo and Hermann began to wonder if they had dreamt it all.

The responsible authorities on Earth and on the Moon were all agreed that the report submitted by Captain Togneri must be somewhat exaggerated, owing to his overstrained condition at the time. A hydrogen cloud might certainly have invaded the Martian Sector. But a solid body? Impossible.

At the United Nations Space Commission in New York, however, it was admitted that something odd did seem to be happening on Spaceway 69.

For some weeks now, pilots on this route had been reporting deviations in free fall, accompanied as a rule by temporary instrument failure. But the reports always included the information that course stability had been re-established quickly by the use of auxiliary jets; and for this reason – and because Spaceway 69 was considered of secondary importance, a route planned originally to accommodate scout and research ships – only an academic interest in the subject was thought to be necessary.

In consequence, the *Ariel* 7 incident changed nothing. As a matter of routine, all captains using Spaceway 69 were again warned what to expect. Then Captain Togneri's report was pigeon-holed and forgotten, both in New York and in Port Imbrium on the Moon.

Only a few individuals like Professor Paavo Salvonen in Finland and Moshe Zack, a young Israeli communications engineer in Port Imbrium, continued to study the problem on a basis of personal interest. Professor Salvonen suspected that some form of magnetism was involved, and as the Earth's greatest authority on the subject he had originated a programme of research which he hoped would either confirm or deny his suspicions. Moshe Zack was simply an amateur astronomer whose hobby, since boyhood, had been the study of books and microfilms dealing with the history of astronomy.

While these two, from different directions, were edging towards the truth, two other men were preparing for a journey.

Thomas Renoir was French – tall, dark and pencil-slim. He had graduated from the Florida Pads as a space pilot, acquiring on the way a reputation for whipcord physical fitness and sharp mental reaction. He had also collected a nickname: Long Tom. Up to date, he had taken part in five space flights to the Moon, twice as co-pilot in a freighter and three times as captain of a research ship. His record was good, though a file in the office of the Space Commission contained a note by one of his instructors: 'Daring. Inclined to be impulsive.'

His colleague was Adam Dominick, a small and graceful Negro with humorous dark eyes and a generous smile. Adam had been born in Zanzibar, the son of a consular official from Nigeria. Though somewhat lacking in operational experience, he had passed all the examinations required of a space captain. On this occasion he was to act as Long Tom's co-pilot, and if all went well with his handling of *Pegasus* 5, he would then qualify unconditionally for a captain's certificate.

The projected trip to the Moon and back of scout ship *Pegasus 5* had a double purpose.

In the first place, she would carry a small payload. This included not only several dozen educational microfilms for Andrew Tyrell, the Englishman with an Oxford degree who supervised education in the lunar colony, but also a crate of radio transistor parts for the Burmese Head of Communications, U Thong, who had been screaming for them in his usual irascible way for weeks.

In the second place, during the flight along Spaceway 69, Long Tom and Adam would collect information about a hydrogen cloud, recently observed approaching and entering the Martian Sector.

As a kind of afterthought, they had also been briefed to find out what they could about the mysterious deviations reported by other pilots.

In the early morning of 15 July 2051, with the Sun peering up over the low hills beyond the Florida Pads, they took their places in a ferry rocket bound for Alpha Main. Accompanying them were fifteen other people. They were the passengers and crew of the liner *Archimedes*, due to leave at midday for the Moon.

When the first queasy moments of take-off were safely past, the Dutchman Vermeulen leant back in his seat so heavily that it rocked in its gimbals. Looking across at Long Tom he spoke through layers of thick black beard.

'Taking over *Pegasus 5*, I am told?'

'Yes. Light freight and reconnaissance. Adam is coming with me.'

'You youngsters have all the luck! Six days' holiday in a scout ship, while I rack my ageing brains and body in *Archimedes*, keeping my passengers happy and maintaining a strict time-table!'

'Ah, but my dear captain' – Long Tom spread his hands, only subconsciously aware of a darkening star-filled sky speeding past outside the ports – 'consider your seniority. Consider how much money you earn compared with Adam and me!'

White teeth gleamed in Adam's black face. 'And consider the strain on *my* brains and body, trying to persuade Long Tom that I deserve a captain's certificate!'

Vermeulen snorted. 'Ach, nobody fails their practical on Spaceway 69. Plenty of room for trial and error. Though nowadays,' he added, with less vehemence, 'there seems to be a problem in the Martian Sector. According to Alf Togneri it is a serious problem.'

'We have been asked to investigate it,' said Long Tom. He added: 'Our principal concern, of course, is the hydrogen cloud.'

A series of muffled explosions cut across their conversation. A few of the *Archimedes* passengers, on their first space journey, looked alarmed, and Captain Vermeulen, as in similar circumstances he had done a hundred times before, spoke quickly to reassure them.

'We have now achieved escape velocity, a thousand kilometres above the Earth.' His words flowed with long practice; the solidity of his voice had an immediate calming effect. 'The motors have been cut off, and we are approaching Alpha Main in free fall. The sounds you are hearing come from the motors. These, as you know, are chemically fuelled, because no atomic drive-unit is allowed by law to operate within a thousand kilometres of the Earth's surface. For the past few minutes they have been running at a temperature of five thousand degrees. Now, as they cool off, thermal contraction is producing a series of small explosions. Everything is normal, ladies and gentlemen. Nothing to worry about.'

Small sighs and smiles of relief flickered round the cabin. Long Tom and Adam exchanged winks. Vermeulen was a rough diamond in many ways, a fierce disciplinarian who could strike fear into the hearts of young crew members with a mere twitch of his bushy black eyebrows. But his unruffled way of soothing timid passengers was an object lesson to junior officers.

The ferry pilot was hidden from those within the cabin by an aluminium bulkhead. Now, only four and a half minutes after take-off, his voice came through on the intercom.

'In a few seconds we shall be alongside Alpha Main. Will passengers please remain in their safety-harness until the air-lock mechanism has been adjusted? A station official will then enter the rocket and conduct you inside.'

Thirty seconds later a slight tremor occurred in the rocket's hull.

Passengers on the port side, glancing out through the tinted perspex, saw a curving mass of grey car on fibre plates, part of the space station's outer shell. It appeared to be stationary.

Passengers on the starboard side had a different picture. Nothing was stationary. Pale stars raced past the windows, and only experienced space travellers recognized that the yellow comet which flashed across their vision every twenty seconds was in fact the Sun.

The illusion was caused by Alpha Main's rotatory motion. Because of centifugal force this simulated Earth gravity in the station itself and in all ships moored alongside.

For years Alpha Main had been circling the Earth every two hours at a height of two thousand kilometres. Its central core, man's original stepping-stone in space had been built and established in orbit before the turn of the century.

Though the first astronauts to reach the Moon had done so by rockets, directly from Earth, it had always been recognized that space travel could only become economical by the use of atomically-powered ships operating from a station outside the Earth's atmosphere. There they could be loaded and fuelled with comparative ease and safety, while a ferry service of rockets linked the station to the parent planet.

Four other stations had recently been put in orbit – Alpha Two, Beta, Gamma and Delta. Alpha Main, however, continued to be the principal 'harbour' for vehicles going to and coming from the Moon. Round its spherical core, as the years went by, there had gradually been constructed a system of 'spokes' connected to a thick and somewhat irregular outer rim. Now it was like a monstrous wheel spinning in space, containing a warren of staff living-quarters, passenger reception rooms, cargo and fuel bays, observatories, laboratories and various other dens filled with scientific equipment which only experts could even begin to understand.

The 'day' of the little artificial world of Alpha Main was about twenty seconds, the time it took to complete a revolution in relation either to the Sun or to any other particular star. Naturally, however, the permanent staff worked to Earth-time.

As the minute-hand on the clock in the main reception room jerked up towards 1200 hours, the passengers for *Archimedes*, who had been drinking coffee and reading rice-paper magazines, began to assemble near the air-lock hatch. Long Tom and Adam had also been drinking coffee, chatting with friends among the staff. Now they left their table and by way of a spiral staircase climbed to the nearest observation platform.

Here the 'window' was an integral part of the station's curved outer rim. Built of reinforced anti-glare perspex, about ten metres wide and two metres high, it gave a panoramic view of a scene which never failed to move both Long Tom and Adam, even after years of repetition.

Their immediate impression was that the whole universe was spinning round them: it required an effort of will to remember it was the station and not the firmament of Sun and stars that was rotating.

Adam said: 'No wonder our ancestors thought the Earth was stationary and that the Sun went round it!'

Long Tom laughed. 'My family has a story about my great-great-grandmother, who lived in Paris. When the first landing was made on the Moon in 1969, she refused to believe it. "American propaganda," she said. "Newspaper talk. If it were possible to land on the Moon, General de Gaulle would have done so long before now!"'

Becoming accustomed to a regular blinding flare of sunlight every twenty seconds, they looked out at the Earth, an enormous blue crescent filling half the sky. Partly hidden by the bulk of the station, it was slowly waxing as Alpha Main sped along the encircling orbit. In half an hour it would be full. Eighty minutes after that it would be invisible, a black disc eclipsing the sun, with Alpha Main in its cone of shadow.

Immediately below the observation port, attached to the station's rim by a cylindrical air-lock, was what Long Tom and Adam had come to see, the dumb-bell mass of *Archimedes*, a slightly old-fashioned passenger and freight liner built in 2042.

Of about 500 tons gross, with radioactive motors in the smaller sphere and room in the larger sphere for a hundred tons of cargo as well as twelve passengers and a crew of three, *Archimedes* had a first-class service record, thanks largely to Captain Vermeulen's skill as her commander. It was a record marred only by a temporary breakdown which had put her out of action for several hours during a passage to the Moon in March 2050.*

Lying off, about a kilometre beyond *Archimedes*, were two other craft, both moving in orbit with the station. One was the slim arrowhead of the ferry rocket which had travelled from Earth less than an hour before. The other was *Pegasus 5*, a triangular scout ship which always reminded Long Tom of a bobsleigh he had once used in the French Alps. Brilliant in a fresh coat of aluminium paint, and already serviced and loaded, she would soon be coming alongside to take them aboard.

There was movement as the air-lock cylinder withdrew from *Archimedes*'s hull and began to disappear into the rim of Alpha Main.

Adam looked at his wrist-watch. 'Dead on time,' he said.

Long Tom nodded. 'Trust that old Dutchman!'

The big 'dumb-bell' slid away smoothly, a grey trail tinged with white issuing from her smaller sphere. Then the grey was

* See *Super Nova and the rogue satellite* by Angus MacVicar

overwhelmed by the white, and *Archimedes* hurtled off into the dark sky, at the precise speed which Captain Vermeulen, with the aid of a computer, had calculated would take her to the Moon – along Spaceway 7, the most direct and therefore the most popular route – in exactly sixty hours.

'Ah, well,' said Long Tom, 'our turn next. Time for de-contamination and suiting. Better go down, Adam.'

'Yes. Better go down.'

Their voices were slightly sombre. In spite of all their train-ing and technical expertise, the imminence of a journey into space still caused them to draw deep breaths and feel a flutter in their stomachs. Out there they would be alone, except for the radio link. Out there they would be exposed to dangers not yet fully understood by the groping minds of men.

2 | Pegasus 5 in peril

INSIDE the dome-shaped cabin of *Pegasus 5* the pale helium lights were steady. Outside, revealed by a wide observation port, starlight flickered in a black sky.

Under the port was a shelved instrument panel. Its dials, grouped around a clock, recorded jet output and speed, temper-atures both inside and outside the ship, internal air-pressures and internal and external radiation levels. The shelf supported a pinging radar screen and a radio transceiver which hissed and faintly crackled.

Facing the port and the panel, less than a metre away, Long Tom and Adam sat side by side in seats of white plastic and foam rubber. Safety harness prevented them from floating about the compartment. They wore regulation space-suits, though twenty minutes ago, soon after take-off, they had re-moved their helmets.

'So far, so good,' said Long Tom, readjusting straps and buckles and settling more comfortably into his seat. 'How are we going?'

Having consulted the chart clipped to a folding table on his left, Adam used the space-range calculator, an instrument which looked like a set-square combined with a spirit-level. It was the invention of Professor Ernst Lindt, Head of SCO, the Scientific Co-ordinators, on the Moon.

As the calibration point settled, Adam said: 'Entering K-lat 9, M-long 98, five thousand kilometres out from Alpha Main, dead on course. Junction with Spaceway 69 in approximately thirty-five minutes.'

'Good. Check with Alpha Main Control.'

Adam spoke into the transceiver.

A voice came back, professionally drab and unemotional. *'Control to* Pegasus 5. *Fix spot on. Nice going.'*

Long Tom looked at the clock. He waited until the second hand had done a complete revolution, then moved a lever on the control deck between them. As the pointer on the jet output dial dropped back to zero, he slotted the steering column into a fixed position. In this type of space-ship the twin power jets aft performed the function of a rudder, swivelling sideways and up and down like an outboard motor in a sea boat. Without power *Pegasus 5* was in free fall, and for the time being, therefore, the steering factor had become irrelevant.

He sighed a little and said: 'Well, Adam, no more worries for half an hour – we hope! Care to take over? Take us on to 69?'

'Sure. Prepare to meet thy doom, man!'

'Remember if I meet mine, you'll meet yours!'

There was no need for them to exchange seats: the steering column and power controls were central. But Adam handed across the charts and space-range calculator, and Long Tom, now assuming the responsibilities of navigator and radio operator, clipped them to the folding table on his right.

The compartment was quiet except for continual small

sounds coming from the compressors and from the radio and radar. As it always did, a faint odour of warm oil and metal tainted the artificial freshness of the 'atmosphere'.

Adam studied the clock and various dials and checked figures on the flight plan suctioned to a board on the control deck. Then he looked out at the staring stars. They had lost their twinkle, because in the depths of space there was no atmosphere to scatter light; but he was accustomed to this phenomenon and therefore undaunted by their glaring enmity. He regarded them now only as guide-marks on a journey, in much the same way as air and sea captains on Earth regarded beacons and lighthouses.

Finally, having satisfied himself that the ship was in good heart and behaving well, he took the log-book from the shelf in front and recorded his take-over as Captain.

For a time there was silence. Tiny sounds appeared to become louder. A knot of tension tightened between the two men.

Abruptly Adam said: 'Everything is normal. *Pegasus 5* is moving with the grace and speed of the mythical horse after which she is named. And yet – I have an odd feeling, Tom.'

A minute ago he had made a joke; his laughter had been carefree. Now, coincident apparently with his acceptance of command, his good humour had deserted him.

'A feeling?' said Long Tom.

'One of my ancestors was a witch-doctor. He lived alone in the jungle yet was famous throughout West Africa. He foretold great wars among the tribes, and those wars happened just as he said. You have read about them, Tom, and about the bloodshed that almost ruined my people. He foretold also that peace would come at last, on the very brink of disaster, when atomic weapons were finally outlawed and all nations and races began to understand each other. Peace came, too, as everybody knows.'

Long Tom shrugged. 'Very interesting. Fine dramatic stuff. But how does it apply to this feeling of yours?'

'My ancestor's gift. Second sight, call it what you will. Do you think I may have inherited it?'

'Ah, now I understand. You have a premonition?'

'Something like that.'

'Well?'

'There is no evidence to justify it. But I am suddenly afraid.'

'You, Adam! Afraid? The guys in Alpha Main reckon you don't have a nerve in your body.'

'This time it's different. We're heading for danger. I feel it in my bones.'

'*Sacré nom!* What kind of danger?'

'I don't know. Nothing is clear. I am sorry, Tom —'

'Oh, snap out of it! A touch of space sickness, that's your trouble. Take a pill.'

'I'll be all right.'

Tom gave a small, uncertain laugh. 'If you go on like this I'll be forced to give you a bad report.'

'I know.' The response was gloomy.

'Well, I don't want to give you a bad report. It would embarrass me. Anyway, you don't deserve a bad report. I've seen you handle a ship before. Like a dream.'

'I said I'm sorry.'

'You and your darned old ancestor. A witch-doctor! This is the space age, Adam; the computer age. There's no room in it for superstitious fancies. Science has taken over from second sight.'

Slowly, during a long pause, Adam's expression began to change.

At last he said: 'I deserved that. Your common-sense makes me feel better.'

'That's a relief! I thought you were sickening for something.' Tom patted his arm. 'Fancy a glucose drink?'

'Sure.'

'*Bien!* Plenty of time to enjoy it before we do our fancy turn on to 69.'

Opening the cabinet beneath the shelf in front, Long Tom extracted two plastic bottles. He tore off the seals, liberating the anchored drinking tubes, and handed one to Adam.

There was no more talk of danger. But Long Tom was uneasy. And in Adam's mind there remained a completely unscientific picture of a hydrogen cloud, in which there loomed a shadow of destruction.

With a brief motor burn accompanied by skilful manipulation of the 'rudder', Adam put *Pegasus 5* into Spaceway 69. Then once again the atomic motors were cut, and the scout ship, in free fall, headed for the Moon like a bobsleigh on a groovy run. Only the tiny service motor, which maintained electrical power in the cabin and cargo compartment, continued to tick over in the lead-lined reactor chamber aft.

Long Tom and Adam settled down to routine, surrounded by the various graphs and record sheets which were so much a part of every astronaut's life. At stated intervals they exchanged a word or two with Alpha Main. As their position in space became more remote, the voice of each successive duty controller grew thinner and less resonant.

At the end of twelve hours Long Tom slept, while Adam remained on duty. Six hours later Adam handed over and slept in his turn.

Before beginning each spell of duty they visited the toilet in the after part of the ship. A piece of standard equipment in every space-craft, this little apartment was a separate unit mounted on ball-bearings. The press of a button made it spin until centrifugal force provided about a quarter of Earth gravity and insured that everything inside moved downwards. Washing, shaving and the natural functions could then be carried out in reasonable comfort and without awkward complications.

During the 'day', at regular times, they had their meals together, mainly processed food out of sealed cartons washed down by a variety of fruit drinks.

For a few minutes every hour, even while at work, they did

their isometric exercises, rhythmically loosening and flexing almost every muscle in their bodies. In the cramped conditions of a scout ship these were essential to normal health.

Occasionally they switched on the television. The programmes they watched were broadcast by the Inter-Stellar Television Authority, via the big ISTA satellite orbiting the Earth a thousand kilometres beneath Alpha Main. They originated from stations as widely separated as New York, London, Moscow, Tokyo, Canberra and Brasilia. Sometimes, on special occasions, news pictures were fed back from Port Imbrium and from the interior of ships in orbit.

During this particular flight, however, the news followed a common pattern.

There had been a row at a meeting of the Space Commission in New York concerning a project to increase the size of Alpha Main; but as rows like this occurred almost every other day, Long Tom and Adam were yawningly uninterested in it. They were both ready to admit, however, that such verbal wranglings were an improvement on the physical strife which had scarred the Earth's conscience in the twentieth century.

A speech had been made in the United Nations by the President of England, pointing out that the Scots had been trading clandestinely with a pirate colony inhabiting the east coast of Greenland, thus violating their Independence Charter of 1987. He demanded the immediate imposition of economic sanctions. At this both men shouted with laughter and began to think up wisecracks for the benefit of Steve Murray, that perfervid Scot, when they met him on the Moon.

Another news item concerned the internationally famous New Zealand philosopher, Gerald Kaye, who for some time had been a vociferous opponent of the new demand for a twenty-four hour week, his argument being that too much leisure brings about human degeneration, both physical and mental. He had been gravely injured in an accident to his private helicopter but had been supplied in less than forty-eight hours with a new heart and a new kidney from the Spare Part Surgery

Depot in Johannesburg. It had now been arranged that he should spend a few months' convalescence in the low-pressure recovery wing run by 'Hughie' Akiziwi, a brilliant young Nigerian doctor, in the Lunar Hospital at Port Imbrium.

On the sports side, the Brooklyn Dodgers had beaten the Berlin Cougars and were now within two points of winning the New World Baseball Series. In Tokyo an athlete from Kenya had beaten the High Jump record with a leap of 2.98 metres. A Peruvian footballer called Eucadio had been transferred from Montevideo Rangers to Glasgow Celtic for two and a half million dollars, which, as Long Tom remarked, seemed finally to dispose of the legend of Scots meanness.

Battened down under muffling hatches of work, Adam's premonition was not discussed again. Indeed, as *Pegasus 5* entered the fourth day of her journey, still travelling at approximately 29,000 kilometres per hour, his uncharacteristic outburst had been almost forgotten by them both.

At 0700 hours on this fourth day they were approaching the Martian Sector, only eleven hours out from the Landing Ground on the Moon. Adam shook Long Tom awake, believing it to be the last time he would do so on the present trip. After a breakfast of lemon juice and egg cake, they began to prepare the instruments they would require during the next three hours, a period crucial to their study of the hydrogen cloud.

What astronomers call 'clouds' in space are so tenuous that they are invisible to a human eye and can be detected only by radio telescopes, radar and other highly sensitive devices. They consist generally of wispy whorls of hydrogen gas, though sometimes other scraps of interstellar matter are discovered in their midst.

Tentative calculations had already revealed that this particular cloud was spherical in shape, with a diameter of some 10,000 kilometres, and that from the point of view of the radio telescopes at Green Bank, Maryland, Jodrell Bank in England and Kuybeshev in Russia, it was peculiarly 'opaque' and had a core of abnormal density. Furthermore, as compared with the radiation emitted by ordinary clouds of cold, rarefied hydrogen on a constant wavelength of 21.1 centimetres, it had been discovered that the wavelength of radiation emitted by this unusual specimen varied from 18.3 to 30.2 centimetres, as if some kind of magnetic influence were at work.

It was hoped, however, that the crew of *Pegasus 5*, by employing a battery of scientific aids built into her hull and by operating three analysis probes, would be able to record sufficient data for the experts to make a more detailed assessment of its area and composition.

Long Tom and Adam reckoned that the whole investigation could be carried out in roughly fifty minutes, the approximate time it would take to shoot the three probes through and beyond the cloud and bring them back.

At 0800 hours, by which time all their preparations were well advanced, a voice crackled in the transceiver. '*Alpha Main calling* Pegasus 5. *Are you reading me? Over.*'

Long Tom lifted the mouthpiece. He said: 'Pegasus 5 to Alpha Main. Reading you sharp and clear. Ship and crew A-okay. Position B-lat 7, A-long 89. Do you read me? Over.'

'*I read you. Radar confirms your position. Latest information on hydrogen cloud puts it at B-lat 3, A-long 95, approximately fifteen thousand kilometres west-north-west Spaceway 69. Commission gives approval for detour, if necessary. But look out for deviationary effects and possible instrument failure. Over.*'

'Roger. Our heads are down, eyes on the ball.'

'*Handing you over now to Lunar Communications, as per schedule. They'll talk you in. Okay?*'

'Okay.'

'*Good hunting. Mind your step. Over and out.*'

Long Tom adjusted the wavelengths. Then he remarked to Adam that to be a controller in Alpha Main had long been his ambition. 'Just imagine: four-hour duty spells and steak and eggs for breakfast every morning!'

Adam chuckled. 'Don't kid yourself, man. You're a space pilot. You'd die of boredom stuck in Alpha Main, in spite of the steak and eggs.'

'If you mention steak and eggs again, you can whistle for your captain's certificate!'

'So! You mentioned them first!'

It wasn't an argument, merely the fragile small talk of astronauts cooped up together for days at a time.

The exchange was cut short by a flurry of sound from the transceiver.

'*Lunar Base calling* Pegasus 5. *Are you receiving me? Over.*'

Long Tom smiled across at Adam. 'That's Steve Murray. I'd recognize his accent anywhere.' He spoke into the mouthpiece: '*Pegasus 5* to Lunar Base. Reading you loud and clear. Salutations, my old Scotch thistle! How did the haggis taste this morning? Over.'

'*Better than frogs' legs, you skinny Frenchman! We have you in the radar, position B-lat 4, A-long 93. Check.*'

'Check. In a few minutes we may move out of Spaceway 69 to have a closer look at the hydrogen cloud. Keep an eye on us. Over.'

'*Wilco. Good luck, Tom. Tell Adam we have a party laid on for him when he gets that certificate. Over and out.*'

They traded smiles. Conversation on the radio would now be more informal, more amusing. Staff in the Communications dome on the Moon were all old friends of theirs – Steve Murray, Moshe Zack, Nikki Charles, Kushi Mohammed, Lars Sorenson. The redoubtable U Thong, Chief of Communications, was also a friend, in spite of his brittle temperament and outbursts of exotic language. They were even allowed to call him by his nickname, which was Whippy: this by association not only with the word 'Thong' but also with his sharp character and wiry physique.

Their journey began to appear less drab and monotonous. Soon there would be some action; and in another eleven hours, if all went well, the trip would be over and they could enjoy themselves in congenial company.

The action came sooner than they expected.

At 0823 hours a faint ping came from the radar, whose beam had been directed for some time at the hydrogen cloud. The bar began to circle through a thin and scattered area of light. In the centre of this area appeared a single shining pin-head.

'That's odd,' said Long Tom. 'Do hydrogen clouds have a solid core?'

'Not to my knowledge.' Adam looked puzzled. 'But this is what Alf Togneri and Hermann Buedeler must have seen! And nobody believed them!'

By 0830 hours the image of the cloud had become larger and better defined. The pin-head had grown brighter.

'I propose we make that detour,' Adam said. 'Circumnavigate the cloud and launch the analysis probes.'

'Okay. Shall I take over?'

'Not unless you particularly want to.'

'I don't particularly want to. Carry on, skipper!'

Adam smiled with pleasure at Long Tom's confidence in his skill. He released the steering column, caressed the atomic motor lever. Jets spouting and slewing, their power imperceptible in the crew compartment, *Pegasus 5* left Spaceway 69, heading west-north-west.

Long Tom described the manoeuvre to Lunar Base. Steve Murray's voice came back, gruff and friendly, acknowledging the message and adding:

'That solid body in the cloud. Sure it's not the egg-cake you had for breakfast? Causing spots before your eyes . . .'

Long Tom's reply was short and snappy and concerned the boorish ignorance of the whole Scottish race. Adam laughed.

At 0910 hours, when they reckoned the ship was still two thousand kilometres from the cloud, they noticed a flicker of pointers on the instrument panel.

'Aha!' Adam's eyes widened. 'The bogy man of the Martian Sector begins to show himself!'

Again a flicker, as if for a split second the power supply had been interrupted.

Steve Murray came through: '*You*'*ve gone all quiet. Not like you, Tom. Any more spots?*'

'Nitwit! There's only one spot, as I already said! And now our dials are on the blink. The usual deviationary effects.'

'*Well, play it cool.*' Steve's humour appeared suddenly to fade. '*That spot of yours,*' he went on. '*U Thong has sent for Moshe Zack. Last night in Recreation Moshe gave a lecture on the history of astronomy. None of us here attended it; but Whippy was told this morning that Moshe mentioned a wandering planetoid which appeared in the Martian Sector eighty years ago. Could be a connection.*'

'Any sensible guidance will be gratefully received,' said Long Tom, dryly.

The transceiver became quiet. As he cradled the mouthpiece, Long Tom caught sight of the speed indicator. Its pointer was flipping across the dial, touching a remarkably high figure on the upward swing.

Anxiously he glanced out at the moving stars. 'What goes on?' he exclaimed. 'The power is cut, yet our speed is increasing.'

'Maybe I allowed too much thrust on the breakaway. I'll let her ride for a minute: see what happens.'

Pegasus 5 moved towards the cloud. The pinging of the radar became louder. The scatter pattern of gas began to fill the screen.

The size of the pin-head increased.

At 0913 hours, reading from the space-range calculator, Long Tom said: 'Five hundred kilometres. Near enough, don't you think?'

'Sure. We'll establish an orbit, then launch the probes.'

Adam had been using the computer to make a series of calculations. Now he transferred his attention to the steering column and the motor lever. Stars flew across the port as *Pegasus 5* did a quick right-angled turn. A few seconds later she was moving parallel to a wispy wall of hydrogen, launched into a giant orbit.

In ordinary circumstances she ought now to have maintained her new course around the cloud in free fall, with only an occasional corrective use of the jets. A moment after the power was cut, however, both men realized that she was yawing rapidly to port and moving towards the cloud. The pin-head on the radar was suddenly a glowing blob, its ping as resonant as a bell. Rushing stars provided visible evidence that their speed was increasing at an alarming rate. The external hull temperature pointer began to sweep up across the dial.

Long Tom said sharply: 'Get out of it, Adam! Turn away!'

But Adam's hands, reacting to the same quick instinct of danger, were already busy. The scout ship swung, stars flashing in the port. At three-quarter power she headed away from the cloud and the thing within it.

She headed away; but in relation to the cloud all avoiding motion ceased. She hung and hovered in orbit and the stars were almost still.

'*Bon dieu!*' Long Tom was watching the jet output pointer flickering on 75: sweat glistened on his forehead. 'We're hooked! Some kind of gravitational and magnetic influence . . .'

Adam's face, too, was agleam with sweat. His mouth was open, thick lips slack. He had a mental picture of the rapidly emptying tank which supplied the droplets of water to the atomic jets. He had another of *Pegasus 5*, bereft of power, being dragged back relentlessly towards an undefined source of destruction.

Long Tom spoke volubly to Lunar Base. There was no answer.

In a tight voice he said: 'Adam, the signal's gone! The radio signal from the Moon. There must be something – a solid body blanking us off.'

But Adam was listening with only half his mind. He had been struggling to decide between two evils. Now, affected by

Tom's anxious words, he made his decision and thrust down on
the motor lever. The jet output pointer swung and stuttered up
to 100. Slowly the stars began to move, as if the anchor chain
which held the ship had become elastic.

The two men held their breaths. Speech between them was
impossible in this time-lock of decision. If they were caught in
a gravitational field, had they sufficient power to achieve escape
velocity? If not, what would be their subsequent fate?

The answer to the second question was fairly obvious. As
long as the jets functioned they would be able to maintain their
present orbital position. When the water tank emptied and the
power failed, however, they would be hauled down in great
circular sweeps, like a hooked salmon on a line, until at last
Pegasus 5 made contact with the unknown source of energy in
the cloud. Whether this contact proved to be violent or relatively gentle would depend on how the ship was handled
and on the natural forces involved. In any case, there could
be only a slender chance that either of them would survive it.

Their intention of using the analysis probes and other
scientific aids was forgotten. All their mental and physical energy was concentrated on the grim situation that had occurred
with such apparent unexpectedness.

Had they taken time to ponder, however, they would have
realized that it had caught up with them in a subtle sequence of
events which they – and other more competent observers on the
Earth and on the Moon – ought to have recognized as
significant long before it was too late. The reported deviationary effects, for example, should have suggested a large
astral body somewhere in the vicinity of the Martian Sector.
The flicker of the instrument pointers should have indicated a
source of magnetism in this body similar to that in the core of
the Earth.

But was it too late? *Pegasus 5* was drawing away from the
cloud. Automatically Long Tom kept reading from the space
range calculator: 'Two hundred metres. . . . Four hundred. . . .
Eight hundred. . . . Twelve hundred . . .'

The elastic band was stretching. Ordinarily the scout ship never used maximum power, and the slight thrusts required for manoeuvring in space consumed water only in small quantities. On her last journey to the Moon, for example, she had returned to Alpha Main with her two-hundred gallon tank still three-quarters full. But now, at full throttle, the twin jets were hurling out droplets of water at the rate of three gallons per second which would empty the tank in less than two minutes.

Two minutes. If at the end of two minutes *Pegasus 5* had still not escaped from the unknown influence, Long Tom and Adam would face almost certain death.

3 | Distress call

PORT IMBRIUM on the Moon, situated under the white-streaked pinnacle of Piazzi Smyth, was a collection of air-tight domes set starkly against splintered rock formations and narrow, ash-carpeted valleys. On every side geometrical cliffs came thrusting up from curving black horizons.

On the highest level eight small domes provided accommodation for the unmarried colonists. In the lunar community they were known as the Bachelors' Buttons. Immediately below them, sixteen similar domes made up the married quarters. Benedicts' Row had been built in a semi-circle, at the hub of which were three larger domes – the School, the Recreation Hall and the Hospital.

On the lowest level, adjacent to the flat Landing Ground with its Transport Hangar and floodlight pylons, were four other domes of irregular size. Generally referred to as City Centre, they contained the offices and technical equipment of the Administrators, the Scientific Executives, the Scientific Co-ordinators and the Communicators. Above the green plastic canopy of the second towered the barrel of a high-powered telescope. Outside the last was a constantly circling radar-bowl and a slender radio-mast a hundred feet tall.

On each level, situated centrally relative to the domes, were grey, rounded structures less than two metres high. These were the thick leaden roofs of the flare shelters – artificial caverns each capable of containing a hundred personnel. Roughly every two years the sun showers energy particles and radiations into space, and anyone exposed to them in airless conditions, even though wearing a vacuum suit, is in danger. A constant watch was kept on the sun by the Scientific Executives, and when a violent flare was observed a radio alarm was broadcast. The colonists had then to move quickly to the nearest shelter, because the first radiations were liable to strike the lunar surface only ten minutes later.

The Moon's 'day' lasted a fortnight, its 'night' the same length of time. As in Alpha Main, however, and as in all satellites and voyaging space-ships, its official time was Earth time.

In the lunar environment 'daylight' and 'darkness' had little relevance. Work and recreation generally took place within the domes, where air, light and temperature, regardless of conditions outside, were always of the same quality. The men and women who had to work or travel outside the domes always did so in vacuum suits. It made no difference to them, therefore, whether the lunar temperature was $100°C$ at 'midday' or $-200°C$ at 'midnight'. And if it was dark they merely switched on their helmet lights and continued to carry out their functions with undiminished skill.

At 0914 hours on the morning of 19 July, the exterior aspect of Port Imbrium was still and lifeless. The domes were pale green mushroom growths, their elongated shadows etched sharply against the ash-bright background. Small tracked rovers stood in orderly lines in two laagers, one convenient to both the Bachelors' Buttons and Benedicts' Row, the other to City Centre. Above the colony loomed the limitless canopy of space, like a soundproof dome of black velvet decorated with a glowing sun and unwinking stars. Piazzi Smyth partially concealed the crescent Earth, blue, cold and enormous. The whole vista resembled a drably-coloured technical sketch devoid of vitality.

Within the domes, however, there was plenty of life. Housewives attended to household chores. Children at school chewed their scripto pens. Men and women were busy in all four domes at City Centre – and had been since 0800 hours, one of the key 'change-over' times. Others not on duty were either asleep in their living quarters or enjoying time off in the Recreation Hall.

Suddenly the dead external picture was invaded by movement. From A-dome in Bachelors' Buttons there emerged a broad space-suited figure. It hurried towards the transport laager, climbed into a tracked rover and, through an atmosphere so rare as to be soundless, set it in silent motion towards City Centre. There the figure dismounted and at a shambling run approached the big dome under the radar-bowl and radio-mast.

Inside Communications a kind of normality existed. The green-tinged semi-transparent plastic of the dome, designed to withstand not only the impact of meteoric dust particles but also great extremes of heat and cold, filtered the oblique sunlight to an even glow. As in every other lunar dome, a complicated machine powered by sun-charged batteries and known as the Equalizer automatically maintained an atmosphere similar to Earth's in respect of pressure, humidity, temperature and oxygen content.

Moshe Zack, whose native city was Jerusalem, came in through the air-lock and breathlessly divested his stout body of helmet and vacuum suit. Three of his colleagues were seated at the central control desk with its broad panel of dials, screens and winking lights. One was Steve Murray, on traffic control duty. Another was Kushi Mohammed, the handsome, bell-voiced Pakistani whose job at the moment was that of local message clerk and Earth-link operator. The third was U Thong, otherwise known as Whippy, small, beady-eyed and slightly wizened, who for the past ten years had been Head of Communications.

Now revealed as wearing regulation white overalls, Moshe lumbered towards them.

Whippy screamed at him: 'Ministering angels, defend us! Were you so dazed with slumber and sloth that it has taken you five minutes to make the journey here from A-dome?'

Moshe decided not to waste time and energy in pointing out that he had gone off duty only an hour before and that Whippy's imperative summons on the interdome radio had disturbed him in the middle of his breakfast. Wiping sweat from his forehead, he said: 'What is the emergency? You spoke of my lecture, of my reference to a planetoid –'

'Quiet, please!' Steve Murray's red hair was in spikey confusion. His shoulders were hunched, his broad, dour face was thrust forward to within inches of the radio. Whippy, Kushi and Moshe were jarred by the anger and anxiety of his voice.

He spoke urgently into the mouthpiece, repeating words he had already used three times in the past minute: 'Lunar Base calling *Pegasus 5*. Are you receiving me? Over.'

But still there was no reply: nothing but the crackling sounds of space. He banged his fist on the desk.

'Tom and Adam?' Moshe's brown eyes had widened.

'Tom and Adam,' Whippy said, his snarl tempered with concern. 'Something has happened. Five minutes ago Tom reported they had left Spaceway 69 to investigate the hydrogen cloud. A solid core was showing in their radar, their instruments were on the blink. That was when I called you. Since then – nothing.'

In his precise way Kushi said: 'There has been an interruption of signal. A physical obstruction is suspected.'

Moshe was perturbed. He was also puzzled. 'But how does my lecture come into it?' He spread his hands.

Steve remained crouched forward, listening with his whole

body. Out of the side of his mouth he said: 'You mentioned a wandering planetoid, so we've been told.'

Whippy snatched up a chart from the desk and stabbed with a jerky finger. 'Could your ruddy planetoid now be in this area, B-lat 3, A-long 95? Could it in genuine truth be hidden in what they call a hydrogen cloud? If so, we reckoned you ought to speak to Tom and Adam: advise them on appropriate avoiding action.'

Moshe's big face crumpled. 'I am not sure. I am not a professional astronomer. But the so-called hydrogen cloud could be an "atmosphere", concealing a planetoid within it.'

Ignoring their conversation, Steve made another call to *Pegasus 5*. Again there was no response.

Whippy turned to Kushi. 'Get New York. Make it quicker than a woman's tongue. Ask the Commission what they think about Moshe's theory.'

'Yes, sir.' Kushi lifted the Earth-link receiver.

'Rod Bueno must be told about this.' Whippy used a bayonet plug to connect himself with the dome in Benedicts' Row occupied by the Chairman of the Lunar Council. Sharply he added: 'Steve, you keep calling. *Pegasus 5* cannot have vanished like a fairy's ghost. Beam the radar on the hydrogen cloud. You may pick up something.'

Pegasus 5 was straining to break the invisible elastic of magnetic and gravitational pull.

A pale film of mist began to form on the outside of the observation port. Long Tom and Adam were aware of it; but the tension racking their minds and bodies prevented them at first from recognizing its significance.

Though the two minutes were now almost gone, the ship was still heading away from the cloud centre; the jet output pointer remained trembling on the 100 mark.

Adam kept pressing down on the motor lever, as if by the sheer strength of his arm he could maintain thrust in the jets. Into the mouthpiece of the transceiver Long Tom called and

called again: '*Pegasus 5* to Lunar Base. Do you read me? Over.'
He did it by instinct. He no longer expected a reply.

Then, with throat-constricting suddenness, the jet pointer
fell back. It still flipped a little, but only fractionally above
zero, indicating that the water tank was empty.

As soon as the fuel supply failed, the atomic motors automatically cut out. With reluctance, almost with incredulity,
Adam took his aching hand from the now useless motor lever.
In his brain was a miasma of terror. It was a terror of the
unknown, like the terror of his ancestors lost in a jungle swamp
with exhalations of evil rising on every side and blinding them.
Desperately he struggled to pierce the fog and think straight.
He was the captain. Quick decisions had to be made which
were his responsibility.

He saw stars moving across the port, stars which were now
oddly on the verge of twinkling. He felt a slight stagger in the
motion of the scout ship and for the first time for days was
conscious of his weight in the plastic seat. He noticed that the
temperature pointers were leaping still higher.

A shock of understanding restored his faculties. His ability
to observe and deduce returned.

The film of mist on the port, the near-twinkle of the stars,
the shudder in the hull accompanied by a rise in external temperature, his sudden awareness of his own weight – they could
mean only one thing. The cloud into which the ship was plung-
ing must surely be different from any normal variety. It must
consist of more than hydrogen. It must, in fact, be an atmosphere, thin and tenuous, no doubt, and nothing like as dense as
the Earth's, but at the same time far more palpable than that of
the Moon. Almost certainly it was the covering envelope of a
spatial body: a body possessing a strong gravitational influence
and therefore of considerable size; a body, too, with a magnetic
field powerful enough to affect instruments at a distance.

Thus, in a moment of truth, did Adam reason. He saw death
approaching as *Pegasus 5*, in huge decreasing circles, swept
down towards the invisible 'world' at the heart of the cloud. But

the very fact of the cloud's composition offered a glint of hope. He could still do something that might delay death, that might even cheat it altogether.

Pegasus 5, like many other ships of comparable design, was fitted with folding wings. As a rule they were retracted inside her flat keel. She operated for most of the time in space, where wings and other orthodox steering attachments – which depend on air friction for their proper functioning – were irrelevant. But at stated periods *Pegasus 5* and her sister ships were re-called to Earth for checking and modification, and at such times they used their wings, both of which were fitted with a set of wheels, to make a safe glide landing near the Florida Pads. Each wing contained a small non-atomic motor which powered braking and lifting jets and made the ship easily manoeuvrable, while the problem of frictional heat on entering the Earth's atmosphere was overcome by a carbon fibre hull capable of withstanding a temperature of 1500°C. After overhaul, the scout ships were returned to space in a capsule attached to one of the big service rockets.

The retractable wing principle had been incorporated in the design of many ships for a less obvious but equally important reason. In the event of some unexpected catastrophe either in one of the space stations or on the lunar surface they could be used to evacuate survivors directly to earth. *Super Nova,* the space life-boat stationed on the Moon, had recently been fitted with retractable wings for the same purpose.

Adam's recognition of an 'atmosphere' outside the ship was followed in the fraction of a second by a decision to use the wings and their small jet motors in an effort to control her headlong tumble to destruction.

He stretched forward and pressed a red stud above the instrument panel. Visible through the wide port, silver wing-tips slid out and locked into position on either side. He pulled a small lever beside the stud. The jets kicked, and with relief he felt the ship settle on an even keel.

Still gripping the transceiver mouthpiece, Long Tom had

been watching his friend's swift movements. Now he nodded approval, though his eyes were still wide with a terror which was taking longer to pass than Adam's.

He was about to make yet another despairing call to Lunar Base when without warning the transceiver crackled and came to vigorous life. '*Lunar Base calling* Pegasus 5. *Are you receiving me? Over.*'

It took him only a moment to realize that the scout ship, under Adam's guidance, had achieved a wide spiral of descent and was now temporarily clear of the 'shadow' of the cloud centre and in direct radio contact with the Moon. Then he began to speak, describing their predicament and its probable cause. Eventually, after about an hour's intermittent conversation, Steve Murray's voice at the other end was cut off in mid-sentence as the ship again became 'eclipsed' by the obstruction.

Each time *Pegasus 5* emerged from the 'shadow', Long Tom and Steve exchanged long messages while Adam, in a cordoned-off world of concentration, battled to retain control of her downward flight.

At last, however, there was little coherence in their talk. Long Tom caught muffled snatches of advice and encouragement and part of a message from Moshe Zack – something about a planetoid hidden in a gaseous envelope, a planetoid that had crept in from outer space without astronomers being properly aware of it. In the circumstances this gave him no comfort, though the anxious voices of his friends did help him to endure the agony of uncertainty.

And suddenly even the voices were no longer with him, obliterated by a savage hiss and crackle in the transceiver. The radar screen was filled by a great blob of light, ringing like a church bell gone mad. Every dial on the instrument panel became blurred by a flickering pointer. The lights in the cabin blinked in and out, in half-second pulses. The ship itself was shuddering, so that he and Adam were thrown about in their harness.

Thin vapour trailed past the port. No stars, no sun: only vapour. Wing-tips vibrated, lifting and falling. For the first time during the voyage there was an external sound: the thin scream of displaced air.

Then, under the vapour, Long Tom saw grey hills and chasms. One minute the splintered landscape was shadowed by 'cloud', the next it shone in brilliant sunlight. On the quickly curving horizon, away to starboard, there appeared what looked like glittering water.

Like a man dazed with blows and not knowing whether it would be heard or not, he croaked out a final message to the Moon: 'We see land. Grey rocks, tiny isolated pools on the horizon to starboard. We are going down.' Then he added the distress call that for more than a hundred years had been recognized on Earth and in space: '*M'aidez! M'aidez! M'aidez!*'

The words impinged on Adam's concentration. He, too, caught sight of the grey forbidding territory with which, in a few moments, they must at last make contact. But the prospect caused him no added fear. Instead, it stiffened his resolve to play out this fantastic game to its end.

The value of his long, keenly-disciplined training as an astronaut was now tested and proved. Tendrils of panic were thrust aside. Tension drained away, and a feeling of calm came to him. He formed a sharp mental picture of what to do.

Into the whining, ringing cacophony he thrust an imperative word: 'Helmets!'

He snatched his own from a hook in front and fitted it on, going through the normal procedures for testing oxygen-supply, heat-exchanger and pressure accumulator, as if there was no emergency. He was glad to observe Long Tom doing the same.

Switching on his helmet radio, he cleared his throat. In a composed voice he said: 'We are now on manual control. I intend to fly her down, as if landing on Earth, though it will have to be done visually and without the help of instruments. We have a chance, Tom. But say your prayers.'

'Nice work, Adam. In case we don't make it, I want you to know that last night, when you were asleep, I radioed a message to Alpha Main Control recommending you for a captain's certificate.'

'Thanks, man.'

There was no further talk. Adam's gloved hands were busy with the controls. Wing flaps moved. Red tongues of braking power erupted from the non-atomic jets.

The scarred and barren land came riding up to meet them.

4 | The secret of Dr Zaeyan

Taped extract from a lecture given by Moshe Zack to the Lunar Astronomical Society on 18 July, 2051:

'... AND while on the subject of astronomical history, I should like to mention the work done by a twentieth-century Syrian astronomer, Dr Nureddin Zaeyan. His home was in Damascus, which, incidentally, is the oldest continually-inhabited city on Earth, having been in existence for almost 4,500 years. His family carried on a lucrative cotton-broking business, and he was immensely rich. He built a private Observatory in the hills above the Krak des Chevaliers, where the ruins of a Crusader fort are still to be found, well preserved in the thin, clear air.

'Though a dedicated astronomer, Dr Zaeyan was also an eccentric. He employed only three male assistants and two female secretaries and was loath to co-operate or share his findings with other astronomers. Indeed, no unauthorized visitors were allowed near his Observatory, which was surrounded by an electric fence.

'Occasionally, attracted by the bait of free computer time at mosphere consisting not only of hydrogen but also of other gases like oxygen, nitrogen, carbon dioxide, helium and argon, as well as water vapour. This holding-down of an atmosphere provides further proof of a strong gravitational force at work.

'Hermes, another of the "male" group of planetoids, frequently approaches to within half a million kilometres of Earth. Dr Zaeyan calculated that Saladin's orbit is so eccentric – probably on account of a prehistoric gravitational brush with Mars – that it spends most of its time on a huge, eliptical orbit which takes it millions of kilometres "beyond" the sun and approaches Earth only once in every eighty years. When it does, however, for some weeks it is less than 300,000 kilometres away.

'Dr Zaeyan discovered Saladin in 1971. This year, therefore, if his calculations are correct, it should again be close to the Earth – and also to us, here in the Moon – following an orbit which temporarily invades the Martian Sector.

'Dr Zaeyan's notes include a possible explanation of why Saladin remained unknown until 1971.

'In 1891, on its previous near approach, radar and radio telescopes were unknown on Earth. Through an ordinary telescope, on account of Saladin's comparatively small size and enveloping atmosphere, an observer would see it only as a vague smudge and be inclined to dismiss it as a trick of reflected light. Even in 1971, with the aid of modern instruments, Dr Zaeyan himself was able to stipulate a solid core to the "smudge" only by means of mathematics.

'Rather dryly he remarks in his notes that at the time other astronomers tended to be "moonstruck" and might therefore fail to notice this tiny sapling in a celestial forest stretching to incredible horizons. His forecast was correct.

'I am afraid the same kind of thing happened in 1994. At first, Dr Zaeyan's "find" was regarded as a major feat of astronomy, but in a year or so scientists seemed to forget about it in their efforts to build metaphorical bridges to the Moon and the planets. I have yet to discover a book on astronomy written within the past fifty years which makes more than a passing reference to Saladin. Not one mentions the prediction that it will come close to the Earth this year.

'You may now be asking yourselves why the good Doctor should have devoted so much time to the discovery and study of a planetoid which, on the face of it, is relatively insignificant. Here romance enters the story.

'It appears that Dr Zaeyan was a devout Moslem and paid regular visits to the Omayed Mosque in Damascus. On one of those visits the Mosque Librarian showed him a holy book printed in the eighteenth century. It was a pot-pourri of Mohammedan legends; and one legend in particular, as the librarian had suspected, appealed to him at once.

'It told of a "friendly star" which spent most of its existence in Paradise but which returned to Earth every eighty years, in case the inhabitants might require its services. According to the holy book, which Dr Zaeyan describes as having an odd apocalyptic flavour, like the Book of Revelation in the Christian Bible, the ancient people of Earth made pilgrimages to it, travelling on "wings of light" or in "chariots of fire". "And in palaces of ice", the legend concludes, "the mighty ones live on in the heart of the star, safe from terrestrial onslaughts of fire and flood, awaiting resurrection".

'A quaint way of describing a pagan heaven, perhaps. But the legend made a vivid impression on Dr Zaeyan, and it is not surprising that throughout his unorthodox but distinguished career he always kept one eye open for the "friendly star" and that eventually he found it.

'In recent weeks I have found myself wondering if the curious experiences of pilots using Spaceway 69 may be due to the so far undetected approach of Saladin on its eighty year orbit. I suggest to fellow amateur astronomers that for the time being they abandon their obsession with distant quasars and white dwarfs and concentrate their telescopes, both radio and optical, on a closer prospect. Namely, the Martian Sector . . .'

'But *Pegasus 5* could have landed. Earth landing procedures were in operation.' Whippy's urgent words betrayed a question-mark. 'She *could* have landed,' he repeated. 'Tom and Adam may be alive, even though their radio is damaged.'

Bueno nodded. He was about to speak when the air-lock opened and three men came in, all wearing vacuum suits. They lifted off their helmets.

Professor Ernst Lindt was a German, thin, pale and be-spectacled, in charge of SCO. Burke Malone, Head of SE, the Scientific Executives, was a burly, dark-haired American with a cleft chin. Since her first launching in 2049 he had been cos-coxswain of the space life-boat *Super Nova*. With Bueno, U Thong and Lindt, he made up the Lunar Council of four.

The third member of the group was Norman Grant, who, though on paper classed as a Communicator and a member of Whippy's team, in reality occupied a unique position on the Moon as a news correspondent. Beak-nosed, head set forward on a vulture's neck, he had trained as a reporter on the *Melbourne Argus*. Nowadays his name appeared in so many news-papers and magazines and his face on so many television screens that he had become as internationally famous as the American President. In lunar circles he was known as Norman the News.

As he went to his desk, situated near the Earth-link radio at the left-hand end of the control panel, his 'boss' glared at him. 'Nobody called *you*!' snapped Whippy.

Norman sniffed. 'I was with Professor Lindt when the Chairman telephoned. Collecting data on the new graphic computer in SCO. Routine stuff. This is real news.'

He sat down, only a few feet away from Kushi. Unperturbed by Whippy's snarling manner – few people who knew the Head of Communications well were perturbed by it – he tested his scripto pen on a writing pad, adjusted horn-rimmed glasses and got ready to use his big ears to advantage.

To Lindt and Malone, Bueno said: 'You know some of the facts. *Pegasus 5*, crewed by Tom Renoir and Adam Dominick, left Spaceway 69 at approximately 0830 hours to investigate what was thought to be a hydrogen cloud in B-lat 3, A-long 95. A few minutes later Renoir reported a solid body showing on the radar, along with considerable magnetic interference with instruments. Then, around 0913 hours, the radio signal from *Pegasus 5* went dead. Murray kept calling and at 0918 hours Renoir's voice was heard again, with the news that in his opinion *Pegasus 5* was caught in a powerful gravitational and magnetic field. He gave a number of instrument readings to prove it.'

Steve tore off the top sheet of a pad on which he had noted down a series of figures. He handed it to Lindt.

'At this stage,' Bueno continued, 'the radio signal was being constantly interrupted, as if by the interposition of a large solid body, but at intervals Renoir was able to report not only the presence of vapour but also a shudder effect in the ship, personal experience of a gravitational effect and a rise in external hull temperature. His words were difficult to catch at times, but from the figures he was able to transmit – they're at the bottom of the sheet, Ernst – it seems clear that just as she was about to achieve escape velocity, *Pegasus 5* exhausted her fuel capacity and became hooked on a rapidly diminishing orbit.

'As a last resort Dominick decided to initiate Earth landing procedures, extending the wings and employing manual control.

'At 0922 hours Renoir's voice was heard here for the last time. But only for a second or two. He spoke of grey land and some isolated pools of water on the starboard horizon. Then he transmitted a "Mayday".'

Lindt's eyes appeared big and protuberant behind pebble lenses. They were mirrors of a mind working swiftly, on a basis of figures and cold logic. He reserved comment until the exercise was complete.

The more extrovert Malone despised logic. His warm heart and thrusting personality were immediately translated into words: 'Tom and Adam were forced to crash-land. On an asteroid, on the fragment of a forgotten planet – does it matter what? They're in trouble, Rod. We ought to launch. Right now.'

Bueno said, quickly: 'Before we decide, there is Zack's lecture to consider. You and Ernst didn't hear it, but I did. Moshe, give us a short summary, please.'

Exposed in unexpected limelight Moshe sweated more than ever. But he cleared his brain and throat of shyness and began to describe the discovery and habits of Saladin, Dr Zaeyan's 'friendly star'. While he spoke the control panel buzzed and flickered with a number of calls.

Having disembarked passengers and unloaded cargo the previous 'day', *Archimedes* was now on her return trip carrying half-a-dozen colonists on Earth leave and a cargo of diamonds, sulphur and iron-ore samples. Captain Vermeulen had picked up Long Tom's 'Mayday' and wanted to know exactly and in detail what was happening. Steve gave him a summary of the latest news and then, with relief, handed over the liner and her importunate commander to Alpha Main Control.

He spoke also to other ships in orbit, briefly supplying technical information and warning their captains that during the emergency they must limit their calls to those which could be classified as 'Top Priority: Urgent'.

Routine 'morning' messages came in from the lunar substations concerning rations, medical supplies and vehicle repairs. Before putting callers through to the dome most competent to deal with their business, Kushi told them of the 'Mayday' from *Pegasus 5* and requested their co-operation in keeping radio talk down to a minimum.

Meanwhile he retained a direct line to New York, so that further information and advice from the Space Commission might be received without delay. Through this medium he learnt that broadcasting authorities on Earth were already aware of the distress call from *Pegasus 5*, and he was able to transmit a few scraps of precious information for their benefit.

Moshe concluded his story.

Malone said: 'So what? If this mysterious spatial "body" is Saladin, then it has an atmosphere. All the more reason to believe that Adam was able to land *Pegasus 5* without too much damage.'

'That's what I say!' Whippy's voice was shrill. 'But he and Tom may be injured, awaiting rescue.'

Bueno turned to Lindt. 'Well?' he said.

Moshe, Kushi and Norman the News became still statues. Steve spoke curtly to the captain of a small freighter who wanted landing instructions.

'Lie off until further notice. *Super Nova* launch from Landing Ground under consideration.' Then he, too, waited for Lindt to speak.

The tall German looked frail, but his colleagues were always conscious of steel in his moral and physical fibre. He came from Berlin, where his brilliance as a scientist had been recognized through his invention of the space-range calculator. Some judged him cold and even ruthless, but his skill as a musician specializing in ultra-modern 'pop' betrayed some degree of humanity in his character. His team in SCO considered him fair and utterly dependable.

He said: 'The evidence of radio and radar points to a solid body within the cloud. The presence of vapour, the hull shudder, gravitational effects and high external temperature indicate that the cloud may be an atmosphere. Possibly, therefore, Earth-landing procedures have enabled *Pegasus 5* to make a landing on this "body", which is almost certainly Saladin.'

'That's what we've been trying to tell you!' exclaimed Malone.

And Whippy snarled: 'Sure it is! Why waste time stating the ruddy obvious?'

They were ignored.

Lindt continued, calmly: 'The various descriptive accounts given by the crew of *Pegasus 5*, though scrappy and confused, present a picture of a planetoid with gravitational and magnetic fields of considerable power, though from the figures given it is difficult to estimate this power exactly. On the other hand, it is evident that *Pegasus 5* could have achieved escape velocity had not the supply of fuel to her jets suddenly failed. It follows, therefore, that *Super Nova* with her capacious fuel tanks and unusually powerful jets could approach and land on the "body" without danger and afterwards make a successful "escape".'

'Good!' said Malone. If he were relieved he didn't show it. His attitude was still one of impatience.

'The area in which *Pegasus 5* has probably come down,' proceeded Lindt, 'should prove fairly easy to find. Since Renoir's last message was heard at all, she was then on the side of the planetoid nearest to the Moon. He mentioned isolated pools of water on the starboard horizon – or what he imagined were pools of water. Now, according to the information transmitted earlier by Renoir, *Pegasus 5* seems to have been orbiting the planetoid from west to east, approximately around the equator. Those pools, therefore, are in the southern sector, not too far from the equator. The scout ship is likely to have come down somewhere near them.'

'So?' Bueno's eyes glistened in the green-tinged light.

'I advise launch.'

The Chairman nodded. 'Then we are unanimous,' he said.

Whippy turned, his hand falling like a clamp on Steve's shoulder. 'Signal a call-out!' he snapped.

The tension broke. Malone ran for the air-lock door, putting on his helmet as he went. Norman the News sighed and made a note on his pad. Into the Earth-link receiver Kushi said: 'Clearing for life-boat call-out.' Moshe emerged from his maze of embarrassment, sat down by the control panel and spoke urgently on one of the internal telephones: 'Nikki? It's a call-out. Whippy and Steve are in the crew, so you and Lars had better come at once to help Kushi and me. No breakfast? Too bad. I'll organize coffee and sandwiches. But make it quick!'

Steve had a sudden, unreasoning desire to disobey Whippy's order.

Vividly there came to him a composite picture of *Super*

Nova's crew: Burke Malone, cos-coxswain; Juan Carranza, assistant cos-coxswain; Hans Lissner, navigator; U Thong, chief signaller; 'Hughie' Akiziwi, space doctor; Janie O'Donnel, space nurse; Boris Ignatieff, crewman, and himself, assistant signaller. Regularly they all embarked and took off in *Super Nova* to rehearse space rescue techniques. It was a simple, even pleasurable matter to initiate such practice call-outs. But the real thing was different. He remembered their first service, when a rogue satellite had threatened to destroy *Archimedes*, and when the space life-boat, hastening to the rescue of the liner's crew, had escaped annihilation by only a fraction of a second.

In front of him on the desk was a plastic box from which there protruded a green and red striped stud. When he pressed this stud a wail summoning crew members would sound on closed circuit receivers in every dome in Port Imbrium.

Juan Carranza, the handsome descendant of a line of Spanish aristocrats, would hear it at his work in SCO, where, as second-in-command to Ernst Lindt, he supervised the computer team. His dark eyes would flash with excitement and even happiness, because Juan loved action and believed himself to be a born leader of men.

Hans Lissner had just returned from a spell of duty as site construction supervisor at the Aristarchus staging-post. He would hear it, therefore, in Dome Seven, Benedicts' Row, probably while enjoying a late breakfast with his wife and two young sons. Elsa would stiffen with apprehension, but she would camouflage her fear for the sake of her husband. Kurt, aged eight, would choke on his cereal as he uttered a spate of eager but highly-intelligent questions. Hans junior, two years younger but with a more placid temperament, would look up and listen and nod a small dark head. Hans himself, like his wife of German Jewish stock long resident in America, would smile at his family and with the patient discipline of his race hide his reluctance to leave them.

Boris Ignatieff, the youthful blond Russian with the wrestler's physique, would hear it in ADMIN, where he was responsible for checking and, if necessary, acting upon the daily reports of atmospheric conditions within all domes in the colony. He would shrug and smile his unexpected smile and tell the anxious girl secretaries not to worry: in all likelihood the emergency was so trivial that *Super Nova* would be able to return in an hour or so.

In the hospital the warning wail would be muted, so as not to alarm the patients. Nevertheless, Dr Hughie Akiziwi would hear it there, in the middle of his morning round of the wards. The expression on his black oval face would scarcely alter. Looking incredibly young for a man whose title was Chief Medical Executive and whose text-books on lunar medicine were required reading in every university on Earth, he would reassure his patients with a flashing smile, hand over his case histories and temperature charts to his senior assistant, Dr Goldstein, and hurry off to the vacuum suit room.

And Janie would hear it, too: Janie in her white pant suit and nursing cap of white orlon, Janie who meant more to Steve than all the other inhabitants of the Moon put together.

It was mainly on her account that for an irresolute moment he hesitated to press the stud. Her father was a maintenance engineer at the Mount Palomar Observatory in California. From him she had inherited her friendly dark blue eyes, her sense of humour and trace of Irish brogue. From her mother, who proudly claimed descent from one of the Pilgrim Fathers, she had inherited her flair for nursing and the steadfastness of character which had enabled her to endure the rigours of a lunar existence for more than three years. Almost all the young men in the colony imagined they were in love with her, especially Steve.

He thought of Janie exposed to the unknown hazards of an approach to Saladin. He thought also of his parents, who lived in Kintyre, Scotland. At this moment, six hours ahead of New York Earth-time, it would be late afternoon on the farm. The hired hand would be whistling to Shep, the black and white collie, as he brought in the cows for milking. His father would be in the byre, starting up the milking-machine; his mother would be in the kitchen. Through radio or television, they were certain to have heard of the plight of *Pegasus 5* and the possibility of a call-out for the space life-boat. They knew that Steve was one of the crew. They would say little, and the farm work would go on, but their hearts would be with their son.

Steve had volunteered for lunar service while working as a signals engineer with the United Nations in New York. He was quiet and 'parsimonious of passion' as Rod Bueno had once described him in a confidential report. But having known him now for over two years, Bueno was aware that beneath a dour exterior the young Scot was a complex of strong emotions, in which sentiment and an affectionate regard for other people were powerful factors. In the harsh environment of the Moon such factors could easily be overwhelmed by a cold and scientific preoccupation with personal survival; but the Chairman realized that in Steve's case this had not happened. He remained yet another example of the old saying: 'Human nature doesn't change, not even in space.'

At this moment Steve's sentiment was warring with his regard for others. He shrank from the idea that Janie might be hurt or even killed in the life-boat, that his parents might suffer an agony of anxiety on his behalf. On the other hand he was aware that Long Tom and Adam might be lying injured in a wrecked scoutship and desperately praying for help.

His hand began to move. The situation with regard to his colleagues and friends had occupied his mind for less than five seconds. In another second he acted. Burke Malone had scarcely reached the air-lock door, and Whippy was still struggling into his vacuum suit, when Steve's finger stabbed down on the striped stud. Then he, too, got up from the control desk and prepared to make the short journey to the Landing Ground. There, beyond the Transport Hangar, *Super Nova* waited in an enormous lead-lined cavity, ready to emerge and lift off like a shining bullet on her mission of mercy.

6 | Rescue flight

AFTER 2000 hours the Recreation Hall was, as a rule, comparatively empty. Children had gone to bed. Men and women were at 'night' work in the four big domes at City Centre, and those off duty were generally all asleep in the Bachelors' Buttons and Benedicts' Row. Its lively periods occurred mainly in the 'afternoons', when the librarian was kept busy issuing and exchanging rice-paper books and magazines, and early in the 'evenings', when films were shown and there was often music and dancing.

On this occasion, however, even at 2130 hours, it was crowded. Sunglare filtering in through the green-tinged, semi-transparent plastic of the dome picked out scores of anxious faces, where their owners sat in tubular aluminium chairs around a central rostrum. On the rostrum, beside a clutter of film-projection equipment, there stood a loudspeaker. This served the regulation interdome radio, which was kept permanently switched on in case of an emergency such as a solar flare warning or a life-boat call-out. It also served a special set on which signals from space-craft could be picked up, as in Communications.

In the shadows behind the rostrum the complicated machine known as the Equalizer hissed gently as it maintained automatic control within the dome of atmospheric pressure, oxygen content, humidity and temperature. Beyond the Equalizer, in even deeper shadow, was the herb and vegetable garden which was a feature of many domes in the colony. Its plants provided ingredients for fresh salads and were also an important adjunct to the Equalizer in the creation of oxygen. Biochemists were hopeful that in the near future plant life would take over altogether from the complicated chemical system in the Equalizer which produced oxygen out of the plentiful carbon dioxide in the Moon's crust.

But the people talking to each other in lowered voices as they awaited further news from *Super Nova* were almost completely unconscious of their surroundings. The diffused light, the hissing heat of the Equalizer's heart, the decorative quality of the garden, the harsh and deadly condition of airless super-heat at present prevailing outside – all those had become so much a part of their existence that they went unnoticed, just as the sough of the sea goes unnoticed by a family living beside it on Earth. In any case, their minds were concentrated on the crew of the space life-boat, now nearly ten hours out from Port Imbrium. Extraneous matters, for the time being, were unimportant to them.

Shared difficulties and dangers always provide the best breeding-ground for comradeship. This rule applied on the Moon, where one false step in the vicinity of a crevasse or the neglect of a single precaution in putting on a vacuum suit might cause instant death, and where survival often depended on the goodwill of another human being. As their predecessors had done, Rod Bueno and his Council did everything they could to foster and maintain this community spirit: a spirit which for almost a century of lunar history had triumphed over differences in language, religion and race and had rendered the establishment of a police force on the Moon an unnecessary and even ludicrous idea. Tonight, the hazardous journey of *Super Nova* brought the colonists even closer together. Members of the crew were in action: those left behind waited and listened and were with them in spirit, offering a firm base for courage.

In the front row of chairs three women sat close together for mutual comfort: Elsa Lissner, Kathryn Malone and Angela Bueno, the Chairman's wife. Leaning against Elsa's knee was her son Kurt. Her younger son, Hans junior, lay drowsing in Kathryn Malone's lap. It was long past their bedtime, but Kurt had refused to go to bed until he knew that his father's navigation had brought *Super Nova* to her target, and Hans junior had refused to go to bed without Kurt.

Behind them sat a subdued gathering of off-duty personnel. It included Andrew Tyrell, the English Director of Education; Renée Debussy, the Chairman's tiny blonde French secretary; Jacques de Smet, a Belgian supply clerk, and Bill Sedibe, who came from Ghana and was a radio maintenance engineer.

On the partition screening off the Library was a large clock motivated by sun-charged batteries. Black hands on a white face, and a slender red pointer below them which smoothly wiped away the seconds, showed the time to be 2140 hours.

Slicing into the muffled talk came the clear voice of young Kurt Lissner. 'Isn't it time, Mother?'

'Time for what, darling?'

'The launch was at 0945 this morning. They have been travelling for eleven hours, fifty-five minutes at an average speed of 25,000 kilometres per hour. This means they have now gone approximately 297,500 kilometres, and Mr Tyrell has told me that as of now *Saladin* is 298,000 kilometres from the Moon. Isn't it time they were signalling back to Communications that they have sighted *Saladin*?'

In form and content the question was remarkable, coming from a boy of eight; but nobody within earshot was surprised by it. Kurt's knowledge of the mathematics and techniques of space, admittedly nourished by both his parents, was well known in the colony. His IQ, according to his teachers, was 'frightening'.

Elsa answered vaguely: 'I don't know, dear. Honestly I don't. Please be patient.' She was thinking about Hans senior in *Super Nova*: in the circumstances a cool answer to a technical problem was beyond her.

But Andrew Tyrell leant forward and said: 'You have forgotten the atmospheric envelope, Kurt. They reported the 'cloud' on their radio some time ago. An actual sighting of *Saladin* may not be possible until they are quite close.'

Kurt nodded, his brow wrinkling. 'I did forget the atmosphere. Thank you, Mr Tyrell.' He might be unusually clever for his age, but in his character there was nothing brash or precocious. His parents, and the prevailing lunar climate of opinion which favoured self-confidence rather than self-esteem, had been responsible for that. In a small voice he added: 'Father is a good navigator. He couldn't possibly make a mistake, could he?'

The lanky, fair Englishman patted his shoulder. 'Anybody can make a mistake, even using a computer. But your father doesn't make many, and it seems certain he hasn't done so in this case. Steve Murray's last report, ten minutes ago, showed that *Super Nova* was on course.'

Kurt sighed. He leant more heavily on his mother's knee and resumed his watch on the clock. The hands were moving up towards 2145 hours.

Reneé Debussy drummed her fingers on a fashion magazine she had been pretending to read. The cover showed a girl in calf-length pants, with a close-fitting yellow satin jacket above a bare waist. Behind her, a little out of focus, a handsome young man in a vacuum suit dangled a space helmet from one finger. Astronauts were still good advertising gimmicks, as sailors had been on Earth during the last century.

Renée said: 'I wish I'd seen Boris before he left. I had trouble with my vacuum suit this morning: the heat-exchanger had to be repaired. When I reached ADMIN he had gone.' Tears spangled her long eyelashes.

Jacques de Smet was small, dapper and dark. He was sad that Renée showed so little interest in him, but against the muscular and glamorous Boris Ignatieff, crewman in *Super Nova*, he knew he had no chance. He said: 'The last thing Boris did before he put on his helmet was to speak about you.'

She clutched his arm, opened her eyes wide and looked up into his face. 'He spoke of me? What did he say?' She was eager, excited.

Like many another before him, he suddenly realized that

when you begin to make up a story unforeseen complications are always sure to develop. In reality, Boris had been far too excited about the call-out even to think about Renée.

Jacques thought quickly. He said: 'As far as I remember, his exact words were: "Renée is late today. When she comes in tell her I'll be thinking about her." '

'Dear Boris!' she said. Then, as an afterthought: 'Dear Jacques!'

Kathryn Malone's blonde hair was piled high. Careful not to disturb Hans junior, she put up a hand to smooth back a fugitive strand. 'I was like you, Reneé,' she said. 'I didn't get a chance to talk to Burke after the call-out. Now I keep worrying about this gravitational and magnetic influence which Saladin is supposed to have. *Pegasus 5* was caught in it. Why is everybody so sure that *Super Nova* will be safe?'

'Rod is sure,' said Angela Bueno, dark-featured and a little plump, a Brazilian like her husband. 'He told me so at dinner, before he and Professor Lindt went back to keep watch in Communications.' She sounded confident, as if everything Rod said must be correct.

But Kathryn had a questioning nature; her faith in science was less blind. Unlike Angela and Elsa and most of the others, she had not been trained for a lunar existence. She had married Burke during one of his extended Earth holidays and had come straight to the Moon from a wealthy home in Brooklyn. 'I know so little of technical matters,' she said. 'I want to understand . . .'

In his brusque yet helpful way Bill Sedibe said: 'Let me explain, Mrs Malone. *Pegasus 5* was caught because her tank ran dry and she was left without power. *Super Nova* has enough water on board to enable her jets to function continuously for at least twelve hours —'

He broke off as a crackle disturbed the loudspeaker. With nervous suddenness the quiet talk in the Recreation Hall subsided.

Then the crackle was transformed into a thin, contained

voice, only faintly recognizable as Steve's: 'Super Nova *calling
Lunar Base. Are you receiving me? Over.*'

The reply came at once, relayed from Communications in
City Centre. Lars Sorenson's voice was loud and incisive. 'Lunar Base calling *Super Nova*. What is your message? Over.'

'Super Nova *calling. Saladin still invisible, though promi-
nent on radar. We have port misting, traces of hull shudder,
slight gravitational effects. Cos-coxswain has initiated wing extension, manual landing procedures. He plans to maintain orbital approach until surface of planetoid becomes visible, then
to make aerial search for casualty before landing.* Super Nova
*and crew continue to rate A-okay. Will call you again soon.
Over.*'.

Kurt whispered: 'Mother, I am saying a prayer that Mr
Renoir and Mr Dominick are still alive.'

Her fingers tightened on his arm.

In Communications Rod Bueno and Ernst Lindt stood facing the control panel. Seated in front of them were the four
men who, with only a few short breaks in the past twelve hours,
had dealt with messages and queries from Earth, from Alpha
Main, from space-craft in transit and, most importantly, from
Super Nova.

At the moment Lars Sorenson, the young Swede who had
won a silver medal at the 2048 Winter Olympic Games, was
maintaining voice contact with the space life-boat. Nikki Charles, the ordinarily gay and talkative son of a famous French
actor, was watching with silent concentration the radar-screen
which picked out *Super Nova* as she began to circle the streaky
maze of light representing Saladin and its gaseous envelope.
His task was to keep the signal in fine focus, and on account of
the great distance between the Moon and the planetoid he was
finding this so difficult that his hunched shoulders ached with
tension. Kushi Mohammed was dealing with domestic calls.
Moshe Zack was as usual in charge of the Earth link.

At a small desk on Moshe's left sat Norman the News, scribbling interim reports for transmission via the Earth link to the Space Commission's news dissemination service in New York.

Once, at 1800 hours, the Chairman made the suggestion that relief operators might be brought in. Reaction had been so cold, not to say inimical, that he had no intention of making it again.

Lars turned. 'You heard what Murray said, sir. Any further message?'

Bueno glanced at Lindt.

The German said: 'I think we ought to report the findings of the Washington computer in regard to the extent of magnetic influence on the planetoid. Also the exact positions where it appears to be strongest on the surface. Burke should be warned not to fly too close to those mass concentration, or mascon, areas.'

'I agree.' The Chairman touched Lars's shoulder. 'Got that?' he said.

'Right, sir.'

'And wish them luck,' Bueno added.

In the spacious cabin of *Super Nova* the physical atmosphere was being maintained at a satisfactory level of pressure, temperature and oxygen content. The moral atmosphere was outwardly calm and professional, though as vapour trails whirled past the ports, causing the wing-tips to lift and drop and vibrate, most of the crew were beginning to feel a surge of excitement. Soon now, if all went well, they might see below them an unknown little world: a world which, after all, might not have proved too inhospitable to Tom Renoir and Adam Dominick. That the two astronauts had been killed was a probability carefully avoided both in word and thought.

All wore vacuum suits, though during the first eleven hours of the flight these had been discarded. Helmets were still not fitted, however: they would be put on only if and when a decision to land were made.

Safety-harness was also in use. During the greater part of the journey it had been unnecessary; centrifugal spin caused by the rotatory jets had maintained artificial gravity within the ship. Some minutes ago, however, the rotatory jets had been cut. At first something like a state of zero-gee had been experienced. Now, as *Super Nova* approached the planetoid on a carefully calculated orbit, the crew were again beginning to feel their weight.

Burke Malone, Johnny Carranza and Hans Lissner occupied the seats at the control desk. Immediately behind them sat Whippy, Janie O'Donnel and Steve. At the rear were Boris Ignatieff and Dr Hughie Akiziwi.

There was a burst of conversation as Steve finished talking on the radio. He waved a gloved hand and said: 'Wait for it! Lars is coming through again.'

The message began with sets of figures which represented the calculations of the Washington computer in regard to the planetoid's magnetism and its source. Steve and Hans Lissner took them down on note-pads. Then came a request for frequent radio information, 'while the going is good'. Currently, as planned, *Super Nova* was on the side of Saladin facing the Moon; but the cos-coxswain was reminded that if she maintained her present course for another fifty minutes she would then find herself 'behind' the planetoid and blanked off as far as contact with Communications was concerned. The message ended with Bueno's good wishes for the success of the service.

Both Malone and Carranza were absorbed in the handling of the ship. The atmosphere of Saladin was clearly not so dense as that of Earth. It had a patchy nature, caused probably by a swirling confusion of warm and cold air currents. Keeping *Super Nova* on a fairly even keel, therefore, was a difficult task which required continuous concentration. But Malone relaxed enough to say: 'Those magnetic poles or mascons, Hans. D'you reckon our present course brings us anywhere near them?'

'No, sir. They point due north and south. We are on a west-to-east course around the planetoid's equator.'

'Good. Right now the flying of this old tub is hard enough without any added complications.'

Malone loved every carbon fibre plate in *Super Nova*: he called her an 'old tub' in much the same way as a man who loves his dog calls him an 'old rascal'.

For some time the gauges on the instrument panel had been dancing. Now the lights began to flicker. Having been warned that this might happen, the crew made suitable mental adjustments.

The radar screen rang and flashed. At intervals Hans called: 'Ten thousand metres. . . . Eight thousand. . . . Four thousand . . .'

The big forward ports were misting over and then clearing with eye-straining rapidity. *Super Nova* trembled, swaying, her wings dipping and lifting. For the first time in their operational experience members of the crew were aware of natural gravitational forces which caused them to be thrown about in their harness and to experience vague air-sickness.

Steve watched from the port at his right elbow. Janie did so, too, leaning across him so that one arm rested on his knees and her dark hair brushed his face. On their left, Whippy glared out of the port on the other side as if daring Saladin to surprise or annoy him.

After thirty minutes Hans announced: 'Two thousand metres.'

Almost simultaneously, eyes bulging at one of the rear ports, Boris Ignatieff shouted: 'I saw something! A second ago, through the vapour. Grey hills and deep valleys.'

Dr Hughie called: 'Boris is right. I saw them, too.'

'Wing braking jets full!'

Malone's order was carried out by Carranza, hands like fluttering birds on the levers.

Carranza said: 'Wing jets full on, sir.'

The vapour outside appeared to slow down. Sunlight blazed through it, then gave way to shadowed dusk.

'One thousand.' Hans's voice was strained.

The vapour cleared. Beneath the ship was a grey land, splintered and riven but with peaks and chasms which, unlike those on the Moon, gave the impression of being weathered into comparative smoothness.

'Cut wing braking jets,' ordered Malone. 'Hold her there.'

Carranza manipulated the controls with the hint of a Latin flourish. A red glow disappeared from the ports, and movement occurred in sections of the wings. The ship became more stable.

'Cut radar.'

Hans acted. The ringing and the flashing ceased. The cabin became quiet except for small sounds of mechanical activity. The winking lights were like ghostly fingers tapping on nerves already taut.

Carranza said: 'Losing height, cos-coxswain.'

'Stern auxiliary jets three and four. Maximum.'

Carranza brought in what represented only a gentle surge of power. The altimeter danced, but the highest swing of its pointer now became constant. He said: 'Level. At eight hundred?' He glanced a query in Hans's direction.

'Check,' said Hans.

Malone nodded. To the crew in general he said: 'I reckon this proves we can land and take off without worrying at all about gravitational or magnetic influences.'

Whippy uttered a neighing sound which might have been a laugh. 'So our tame computer, Ernst Lindt, was right again!'

'Isn't he always?' said Carranza, smiling.

'Like howling Hades!' retorted Whippy, leaving everybody to make what they liked of this unusual comment.

Submerged in a kind of misty twilight one minute and bright with dappled sunshine the next – a phenomenon caused by the cloud formations blanketing the planetoid – the surface of Saladin continued to roll beneath them. Through one of the side ports Malone studied it through powerful binoculars. The monotony of the landscapes which came leaping up from under a startlingly close horizon appeared to be absolute.

Suddenly, however, at the very limit of the horizon to starboard, he caught sight of a tiny flash, like sunlight reflected from a bright surface. It disappeared; but almost at once another occurred in a different place. Malone prided himself on being able to control emotion and excitement; but he found it difficult to do so now. His voice was harsh as he turned to Carranza and ordered a change of direction.

Super Nova banked to starboard, and the little world below her tilted and swayed. A few minutes later she banked again, wings juddering in an area of turbulence. Then she straightened up, now flying on a new east-to-west course, almost a hundred kilometres north of the equator.

Her mouth close to Steve's ear, Janie said: 'I always used to get tummy trouble in an Earth plane. I have it now.'

He put an arm about her shoulders. 'Don't try to kid me! You were never air-sick in your life.'

'Don't you feel squeamish?'

'No. Why should I?'

'I was thinking you looked a tiny bit pale.'

'So to make me feel better you pretended you weren't in such good shape yourself?'

'Well –'

'You're a fraud, Janie!'

He was about to say more; but as he drew in his breath he looked down and saw colour amongst the grey and the words were never uttered. The colour was green, and it formed a circle around a steel-bright pool.

It passed below and was followed by more glinting pools, then by an arid patch of desert which gave the impression that a pot of green pepper had fallen and burst at its centre.

Nobody spoke in the cabin of *Super Nova* until Malone did. Quietly, and with a clearing of his throat, he said: 'I guess this must be the place.'

Eyes strained downwards.

In the rear seat, Boris exclaimed: 'Ahead there, five degrees port, what the heck's that?'

Dr Hughie called: 'Burke, that rock, like a carved pillar . . .'

'I see it.' Malone adjusted the focus of his binoculars.

The ship flew on, with apparent slowness, though her actual ground speed was about 10 kilometres per minute. Situated on the farthest edge of the green-splashed desert, the tall rock came closer. Beyond it, running from north to south, a low cliff was cut out of the jagged terrain as if by the spade of a giant. In the cliff was a series of irregular openings, like caves.

Forgetting to sound irascible, Whippy said: 'What d'you make of it, Burke?'

The cos-coxswain stayed silent. He kept peering down until the curiously-shaped rock had passed below and he could no longer see it from the side port. Then he lowered his binoculars and rubbed his eyes.

Janie whispered to Steve: 'Burke looks awfully tense, doesn't he?'

'What d'you make of it?' Whippy persisted. 'Reminds me of one of those ruddy statues on Easter Island!'

Malone stuck out his chin and said: 'Be your age, Whippy! A trick of the light. There's been weathering here: stands to reason, with a moist atmosphere like this. A good deal more weathering than on the Moon, but not so much as on Earth. Plenty of sharp outlines left, giving slabs and boulders an artificial appearance.'

Whippy decided not to argue. So did the others. But a hush of doubt occurred in the cabin, and for a time nobody looked directly at the cos-coxswain. Steve felt a tingle in his flesh, as if he were on the threshold of incredible danger. Like his crew-mates, however, he did his best to ignore it.

Then, in a flicker of twilight, they saw something else. It lay on a level oblong of desert, not far from yet another shining pool. From the height at which *Super Nova* was flying it resembled a grey moth resting on the ground with wings outstretched.

'It's *Pegasus*!' exclaimed Janie, the only member of the crew who could find words. 'Oh, please, please! Tom and Adam *must* be alive!'

Malone snapped: 'Right, Johnny. Make a tight circle.'

Super Nova came round, tilting and weaving. She was approaching the oblong desert again when a speck appeared on the moth's bright back. There was a sudden flame, and a red star burst into fragments far below.

'A signal gun!' exulted Carranza.

Malone barked: 'Steve, call Lunar Base. Tell them we have located the casualty. One at least of the crew is fit enough to fire a signal rocket. The ground looks good, so we're landing now to investigate. Talk us down, then say we'll get in touch again as soon as possible.'

'Very good, sir.' Steve picked up the mouthpiece.

'Bring her in gently,' Malone told Carranza. 'Cut auxiliary stern jets at two hundred. Then wing braking jets and lifting jets full.'

'Right, sir. Hans, guide me through, please.'

The gigantic shoulders of Saladin widened to receive them. When the driving jets were cut the crew put on their helmets. *Super Nova* sank lower and lower, cushioned on her lifting jets. A cloud of dust rose and enveloped her.

7 | Operation Salvage

THE dust soon settled; but before he moved from his seat Malone ordered a check on conditions outside. This was made possible by the instruments on Hans Lissner's panel: delicate instruments linked to a computer which measured external phenomena such as temperature, radiation and the quality and density of gaseous matter.

When the readings were analysed, the cos-coxswain decided

it would be risky to leave the ship without vacuum suits and helmets. Saladin's atmosphere had a mountain-top thinness, and its temperature in this particular locality was only 3.5°C. Compared with the atmosphere of the Earth there appeared to be a slight imbalance of oxygen and hydrogen. A rather heavy concentration of helium and traces of radioactivity were also recorded.

The atmospheric pressure on Saladin's surface was 1.65 kilograms per square centimetre. Malone instructed his crew to take careful account of this when adjusting the pressure accumulators in their suits. Then he led the way towards the exit hatch amidships. According to plan, and following a routine precautionary drill, Steve, Dr Hughie and Boris accompanied him, while the remainder stayed inside the ship until further notice.

As the hatch door closed behind Steve and he stepped gingerly down the short ladder, he tried hard to keep his nerves under control.

He was taking part in history: the landing of men on Saladin would be proclaimed with tall headlines by Norman the News and others like him. But this was not the real cause of his excitement.

Soon now he would know if Tom and Adam were both alive and well: if they were, he would gain the satisfaction of being part of a team which could bring them back to safety and normality. But this was not the real cause of his excitement either.

He was reckoned by his friends to be a typical Scot; but underneath the dour surface there existed a Celtic imagination which was understood only by people who knew him intimately: people like Rod Bueno, for example – and Janie O'Donnel. At the moment his imagination was teetering on the edge of a wild surmise, conceived by him and brought to birth in the cabin of *Super Nova* whilst listening to his colleagues discussing the pillar-like rock. It was this surmise which threatened to upset the balance of his nerves.

But he disciplined excitement and thrust his imaginings far down under a layer of prosaic calm. He concentrated on the physical problem of coping with a new and difficult environment and of reaching the grounded scout ship, which lay about a hundred metres beyond the towering nose of the space lifeboat.

The problem was tough: Malone, Dr Hughie and Steve were all wearing vacuum suits designed for use in conditions of airlessness and negligible gravity. In consequence, they found that it required great effort to move their lead-shod feet and, indeed, to remain upright at all under the clumsy, clinging weight of the suits and their attachments.

After a short period of experiment, however, they were able to direct fumbling steps towards *Pegasus 5*. Through their visors they saw a similarly accoutred figure shambling towards them.

Steve's helmet radio was switched on. He heard Malone say: 'Who is it? Tom? Adam?'

The reply came in a crackling whisper. 'This is Adam. Thank God you've come! Tom has hurt his ankle, but otherwise he's okay.'

Struggling towards each other, feet crunching heavily on brittle stones, Malone and Adam met and embraced. Steve and Dr Hughie joined them, shook Adam's gloved hands, clapped him on the back. Steve was glad he was wearing a helmet so that the tears in his eyes might stay unseen.

Slowly they went towards the scout ship.

Adam said: 'When we landed, the radio and part of the instrument panel were smashed. But with fuel we could still have flown. This was what kept nagging us. We'd made a safe landing, against all the probabilities, but had no means of knowing if you had heard our "Mayday" or even if you knew our approximate position. Here we were, more or less miraculously intact but prisoners in this ghostly place.'

'Ghostly?' said Steve, quick to recognize an echo of his own thoughts. 'Why ghostly?'

'I don't know. There is an aura of evil. Perhaps Dr Akiziwi can understand. He is my countryman.'

Ploughing along and slightly breathless, Dr Hughie flashed a smile through his visor. 'There were places in the Nigerian jungle which our ancestors imagined were populated by spirits of the dead: I understand that. But those places were hidden in the bush. There's not much here except open desert.'

The subject was abandoned as they reached the scout ship. They climbed a ladder leading up to the hatch above the cockpit. Both the outer and inner doors of the pressure chamber were open.

Malone stood statue-still, looking down. He was shocked by what he saw. In the co-pilot's white plastic seat, Tom Renoir was smiling and waving – *and he was without his helmet.*

The cos-coxswain took a deep breath of balmy artificial air. 'Adam,' he barked through his radio, 'tell him to replace his helmet at once!'

Adam leapt into the cockpit, gesticulating. His mime was immediately countered, however, by a shrug and a shake of the head from Long Tom, who lifted his discarded helmet from the deck beside him and pointed into it.

Adam's voice came urgently through the radio: 'He was forced to take it off. The oxygen-intake valve is damaged: probably another result of the bumpy landing. But it seemed to be functioning normally when I went outside five minutes ago to fire the signal rocket. That's why I didn't bother to close the hatch.'

'Isn't there a spare in your ship?'

'Yes, sir. In the cargo compartment. But because of his ankle Tom couldn't move to fetch it.'

'You fetch it now. Make him put it on.'

'Sure, Mr Malone.'

While the new helmet was being found and fitted, Malone, Dr Hughie and Steve climbed down into the cockpit. Then Long Tom, protected again from the air of the planetoid, switched on his radio.

'Sorry if I scared you,' he said. 'But I nearly suffocated! I attempted to call Adam on my radio, but it was out of action, too. I had to do something. Because of the flying conditions, I reckoned the air of Saladin might be breathable, and so it is. It's cold, but obviously not below freezing point, because the pools we saw coming down are not frozen. It's thin and leaves you slightly breathless, but apart from that . . .' He raised shoulders and gloved hands and left the sentence unfinished.

Malone said nothing about radioactivity or about the super-abundance of helium detected in the atmosphere. Steve knew, however, that such considerations were in his mind and that until a check could be made by Professor Lindt and his Scientific Co-ordinators on the Moon he would be anxious about the effect on Long Tom's health of even a short exposure.

Dr Hughie must have had the same anxiety; but his voice was cheerful as he said: 'Well, that's one little crisis over. What about the damaged leg?'

'I've tried to stand up, but it's no good. The ship skidded when we landed, and my foot caught under the seat.'

'We'd better get you out of here. Across in *Super Nova* you can take your suit off and I'll be able to examine your ankle more thoroughly.'

He had pain-killing drugs in the small box of medical supplies he was carrying; but Steve noticed that he hadn't brought any AR31, the fluid which was an effective antidote not only for electro-magnetic radiation but also, in some degree, for thermal radiation. He would want to give Long Tom an injection of this as soon as possible, and there was a plentiful supply in the space life-boat.

'Right, Tom,' said Malone. 'Steve, give me a hand with him, please.'

At 2250 hours Whippy's voce was heard in every dome in Port Imbrium, announcing that Tom Renoir and Adam Dominick had been found on Saladin, alive and well. He made no reference to Tom's exposure to the atmosphere of the planetoid but added that his ankle was now being treated by Dr Hughie in *Super Nova* and that the state of morale in the space life-boat was, as he put it, 'costhetic'. This was a word invented almost a century before by pioneer astronauts. That it was now old-fashioned and no longer in common use didn't worry Whippy.

In the Recreation Hall Elsa Lissner said:

'Now, Kurt, everything is going well. All the real excitement is over. Isn't it time you and Hans junior went to bed? By the time you wake up in the morning *Super Nova* will be coming back, and I know Father will want you to be nice and fresh to meet him.'

Kurt appeared to have contracted deafness. 'Mr Tyrell,' he said, turning away from his mother, 'could you please tell me what "costhetic" means?'

'It is twentieth-century astronaut's slang. A rough trans-lation might be "spatially in tune".'

'Nobody uses it nowadays?'

'Nobody except Mr U Thong. But he may be giving it a new lease of life, especially if Norman the News puts it in the papers.'

'Do you think they'll be able to breathe the atmosphere of Saladin?'

'That's not my province, Kurt. But we'll know in the morn-ing. After we've all had a good sleep.'

Renée Debussy, Jacques de Smet and Bill Sedibe all began yawning in a marked manner. Kurt wasn't fooled. He knew that like Mr Tyrell they were ganging up with his mother in her effort to get him to bed. He was aware, too, that Mrs Mal-one and Mrs Bueno were both directing persuasive smiles in his direction and that in Mrs Malone's lap his small brother was awake and becoming irritable.

Remembering an unwritten lunar law, frequently impressed upon him by his parents, that no individual should attempt to impose his will on the majority, he gave in gracefully. 'All right, Mother. Hans and I will go to bed. But you must promise to wake me if anything important happens.'

'I promise,' said Elsa.

Matching Whippy's mood, Rod Bueno in Communications signalled back his congratulations to the cos-coxswain and crew and sanctioned a swinging party for Tom and Adam when they reached the Moon.

'Our morale is costhetic, too,' he said. 'With the exception, perhaps, of Norman the News. His is supercosthetic! At the moment he's talking on the Earth-link nineteen to the dozen – giving poor Moshe apoplexy trying to keep it open! – and within a few minutes all your friends and relations on Earth should be hearing the good news on radio and television.'

To Kushi, temporarily unencumbered by local calls, Lindt said with a kind of wonder: 'The Chairman never forgets the human angle, does he?'

Kushi's grandparents in Karachi had often told him about a period in the twentieth century when people had fought with each other not only on account of the colour of their skins but also because of religious differences. He recognized that the consignment of this period to an historical scrapheap was due to men like Rod Bueno, who thought in terms of individual dignity rather than in those of racial and religious rivalries.

In his precise way, he said: 'I expect that is one reason why we have a space life-boat stationed on the Moon.'

'I expect so,' agreed Lindt, as if glimpsing the answer to an obscure problem.

Nikki Charles was still struggling to align the radar. He sighed and said: 'I have the planetoid clear, but against this background I find it impossible to pick out *Super Nova* and *Pegasus 5*.'

'Don't worry,' Bueno said, cheerfully. 'As long as Whippy's voice lasts out, radar is unnecessary!'

'Excuse me, sir! He's coming through again,' announced Lars, flipping to a clean page on his note-pad.

Whippy was now relaying Malone's opinion that it might be possible to salvage *Pegasus 5* and bring her to the Moon. The cos-coxswain proposed to make a thorough technical investigation, which would last approximately an hour, and then decide upon an appropriate course of action. Meanwhile he wanted to know if by any chance space-suits and helmets could be dispensed with on Saladin.

Whippy read out lists of instrument readings relative to the planetoid and its atmosphere. 'Under such conditions,' he concluded, 'would an exposed human body be at risk? Cos-coxswain requests answer as soon as possible.'

'A comparatively simple calculation.' Lindt was studying the figures on the flimsy torn off and handed to him by Lars. 'Tell Whippy I'll programme the SCO computer right now. The answer should be available by' – he glanced at the clock on the control panel – 'about twenty-three fifty.'

His face was pale and thoughtful in the greenish light. As Lars began to talk into the radio mouthpiece, he turned to Bueno. 'Those last few messages, from both Whippy and Steve Murray. Did you notice anything odd about them?'

'Not really. Whippy and Steve were excited, inclined to be emotional perhaps. But that's only natural. They have found Renoir and Dominick. They have landed on a hitherto unknown planetoid and have the opportunity to bring back valuable information about it. No wonder they sound – well, how would you describe it? – a little mesmerized?'

'A good word, particularly in regard to Steve. Just before they landed he said something about a rock shaped like a pillar. As he spoke, his voice was like that of someone in the presence of a ghost.'

'He was seeing a landscape no human eye had ever seen before.'

'I know. But now there is something else: an obsessive interest in Saladin's atmosphere. They have space-suits. For all the time they will be there, why should they contemplate discarding them? I feel they are not being entirely frank with us.'

'Do top scientists have feelings?' Smiling, Bueno patted Lindt's narrow shoulders. He went on: 'Feed your computer, Ernst. Let Burke have the information he wants.'

An hour and five minutes later, in *Super Nova*, the message they had been awaiting came through from Lunar Base.

'On information and instrument readings supplied computer finds no danger in planetoid atmosphere, provided small doses of AR31 are used and no undue physical exertion is attempted.'

Seated comfortably in one of the spare seats amidships, Long Tom said: 'I told you. The air in the French Alps is far more deadly!'

'You're a lucky astronaut,' said Malone.

'Sure. Point taken, sir.'

The cos-coxswain rubbed his chin. He looked round at the nine people awaiting his decision.

At last he said: 'In the past hour, as you know, Juan, Whippy, Adam and I have examined *Pegasus 5*. We are agreed that when a few temporary repairs have been made, principally to her radio, she will be capable of reaching the Moon, where our maintenance staff have the facilities to make her fully serviceable.

'The take-off from here presents the main problem. But again we are agreed that it ought not to be too difficult. We will begin by transferring a certain amount of water from our tanks to hers: enough to enable her to fly. When she is airborne, *Super Nova* will take her in tow, and together we can achieve escape velocity. We have worked out the figures, and they give a wide margin of success.

'After that *Pegasus 5* will slip the tow and proceed in free fall for the Moon. With the help of her lifting and braking jets she should be able to make a normal landing.

'Tom's ankle is badly swollen, Hughie tells me. In consequence he will remain in *Super Nova* during the flight. But Adam insists on carrying on as pilot in *Pegasus 5*, and I can see no objection to this. Juan has volunteered to accompany him.'

Carranza inclined a handsome head in Adam's direction. 'My pleasure!' he beamed, looking lean and gallant and hollow-cheeked, like Christopher Columbus's swashbuckling first mate.

Whippy cut in: 'Attention please, cos-coxswain, sir! A call from Lunar Base. From those fairy-footed chair-polishers! They wish to be advised of our plans.'

'Tell them our plans are under discussion,' said Malone. 'Tell them also to shut up for ten minutes. Not in so many words, of course. Be diplomatic.'

Whippy snarled. He lifted the mouthpiece and barked into it: '*Super Nova* calling Lunar Base. Plans under discussion. Cos-coxswain says will you ruddy well shut up for ten minutes. Over and out.'

There was a burst of laughter.

Malone laughed, too. 'Be diplomatic, I said! You'll get me dismissed. Returned to Earth!'

Having let off some steam, Whippy looked pleased with himself. 'I sure can handle them!' he said, using an idiom that had been out of date for fifty years. And added: 'Don't you worry, cos-coxswain, sir. If they try to dismiss you we'll all resign!'

Ruefully, Malone shook his head. 'As I was saying,' he continued, 'we will carry out a few temporary repairs in *Pegasus 5*. But that will take time: about twenty-four hours we reckon. Only Juan, Boris, Hans and Adam will be involved: between them they have all the required technical know-how. So what do the rest of us do in the meantime?'

He paused, eyes curiously veiled.

Dr Hughie said: 'I should like to examine those pools and the vegetation growing on their margins. There must be hundreds of them.'

'I agree. Their existence may be partly responsible for Saladin's atmosphere.' Malone spoke carefully, as if his deeper thoughts were elsewhere. He went on: 'I have no doubt the Space Commissioners in New York are already planning an expedition to explore this planetoid, while it still remains comparatively close to Earth. In the meantime, however, it would be a feather in Port Imbrium's cap – and a bonus for Norman the News – if we could bring back some samples of water, soil and plant-life for Ernst Lindt to analyse.'

'We should have to be careful about infection from unknown bacteria,' said Dr Hughie. 'But if we all go through the decontamination unit on our return to the Moon there shouldn't be much danger.'

There was another pause.

It was Steve who grasped the nettle. 'That rock we saw. It's a long way back, over the eastern horizon. I've been thinking, sir, could you move the ship, on her lifting jets –'

'I could.' Malone's eyes were brighter now; his chin jutted. 'And I think I will.'

'But – but have we time?' For a reason she couldn't define Janie was suddenly afraid and groping for an excuse to avoid a closer inspection of the pillar.

Bluntly, Carranza said: '*Super Nova* could take you there in ten minutes.'

And Boris put in: 'The cliff behind the pillar might be worth looking at as well.'

Malone nodded. 'Now we know the atmosphere is not lethal,' he said, 'we could dispense with our space-suits, helmets and lead-soled shoes and wear instead ordinary insulated overalls, light-weight gloves and ventilated headgear. This would make it a lot easier for us to move about. In fact, we could do so almost as quickly as on Earth.'

'When do we start?' said Steve, almost in spite of himself.

The cos-coxswain glanced out of the ports. Clouds were thick and dark to the north. To the south and west the sky was clearer, and through a thick haze the sun could be seen sinking down above rocky ridges which looked like the serrated blades of a curry comb. The light was fading into lingering dusk, which provided further evidence of a deep and vaporous atmosphere.

He said: 'It appears Saladin spins on its axis in much the same way as does the Earth. But according to my calculations its 'day' lasts only six hours and its 'night' – here, close to the Equator – about the same length of time. It will be dark in a few minutes. I propose, therefore, that we begin by having six hours' sleep.

'At first light, after breakfast, Juan, Boris, Hans and Adam will collect tools and spare parts from the technical locker and go to work on *Pegasus 5*. I will then move *Super Nova* to the vicinity of the rock which Steve has mentioned and put her down near one of the pools.

'Renoir will stay in the ship to rest his ankle. Whippy will also stay, so as to keep in radio touch with Lunar Base. Janie, Dr Hughie, Steve and I will form the exploration party. First we'll examine the pool and the desert with the green markings, then inspect the rock and the cliff.

'Any questions?'

Though no great lover of physical exercise, Whippy was inclined to grumble at the prospect of being left behind in *Super Nova*. He realized, however, that if he didn't remain in the ship Steve would have to do so, and he was well aware that his assistant wanted to be with Janie wherever she went.

No other objections were raised.

'All right, Whippy,' said Malone. 'Call Lunar Base – and this time, if you don't mind, try to be reasonably polite! Tell them our plans are made. They'll approve of them, I know. Salvage money is involved, and the space life-boat fund ought to benefit. They'll also be delighted at the prospect of getting a first look at the samples we bring.'

Still muttering, this time on the subject of insulting remarks, Whippy put through the call. The reply he received from Lars Sorenson proved Malone's forecast of lunar reaction to his plans to have been correct.

8 | The tall pillar

As they climbed into *Pegasus 5*, ready to begin work, Juan Carranza, Boris Ignatieff, Hans Lissner and Adam Dominick saw *Super Nova* lift off in a cloud of dust. Reaching a height of some hundred metres, she moved away towards the east and in a few minutes disappeared over the horizon.

'Ah, well,' remarked Boris, grinning through the perspex visor of his hood, 'perhaps my ancestors in Russia were right after all. Even on Saladin the world is divided into the proletariat workers and the bourgeois idle rich!'

Hans's sense of humour wasn't particularly keen. Anyway, he was thinking about something else. He said: 'Kurt is going to be disappointed when we don't return today. But I think I prefer to be working here than to be bombarded by his questions about Saladin. Poor Elsa!'

Juan led the way down into the cockpit. As they opened their tool kits he had a distracted air. To Boris he said: 'My ancestors in Spain could be described as idle rich. They were to be pitied. They had time to dream, and dreams always make reality unbearable.'

Boris looked puzzled; but Adam said: 'I know what you mean, Juan. You have a feeling that instead of finding something new and fabulous and strange, Mr Malone and the others are going to find – well, something old and ugly and dangerous. I have the same feeling. I have had it ever since we landed.'

Juan shrugged.

'If you two go on like this,' said Boris, with an even broader grin, 'I will have to class you as intellectuals. And you know

what used to happen to intellectuals in the good old days. They
were locked up!'

For once Hans's thoughts were diverted from his family. He
was troubled by what his companions were saying, though he
couldn't tell exactly why. His cure for uneasiness, however, was
always the same: a stern concentration on work.

With skilled precision he began to unscrew the damaged
instrument panel. 'They will return before dusk,' he said. 'Then
we'll know the truth. Meanwhile this ship has got to be repaired.'

'Good old Hans!' said Juan, cheering up.

Malone chose a place to land where the ground was comparatively free from dust and small loose stones. When *Super
Nova* had settled, he left a few final instructions with Whippy
and Long Tom and then led Janie, Steve and Dr Hughie
through the exit hatch and down the short ladder.

They stood looking about them, breathing in lungfuls of
cold, thin air through the apertures in their hoods. Not far away
was a green-fringed pool, which appeared to be at least two
hundred metres in diameter. Beyond it was the oblong area of
patchy desert stretching for about a kilometre to where the
pillar rock stood under the cliff.

For a few moments they felt slightly dizzy. Then their
bodies adapted to the rarefied air and they began to walk
towards the pool.

Movement was comparatively easy in their lightweight garments. They were aware of an intermittent, exceedingly chilly
wind; but on account of the insulation built into their overalls,
gloves and plimsolls it caused them no great discomfort. They
would have been similarly protected from intemperate heat.

The dusty ground became tinged with green, and moisture
began to ooze from under their shoes. Dutifully they stopped to
inspect the pool. Each one of them was conscious of a desire to
ignore it, an eagerness to acquire as soon as possible closer
knowledge of the green-streaked desert and the pillar and the

cliff. But they were all scientists, trained to collect and examine facts in a logical sequence, and they were careful not even to mention to one another the odd influence dragging at their minds.

From close at hand the pool looked grey and sombre. Its water was deep, and an uneasy tide undulated from right to left as they looked at it.

Malone said, gruffly: 'Well, Hughie?'

'I've been thinking about these pools. I'm not a geologist, or even a biologist, but it seems to me they are surface evidence that water exists in abundance beneath the crust of the planetoid. Millions of years ago Saladin may have been partially covered by water. Then the water began to evaporate – it still does, as witness the atmosphere – and also to seep away into the porous, lava-type rock. Here and there springs occurred, which now force it back up to form these pools. But the pools are kept from overflowing into rivers by natural underground ducts through which the water drains away again. This could account for the slow cross-movement we see: a spring deep down on our right, a draining duct on our left.'

They discussed the theory and could find no serious flaw in it.

But with feminine practicality, Janie said: 'What happens when it rains?'

'I don't think it rains very often,' replied Dr Hughie. 'The ground is too dry, too dusty. There are no mountains and no forests to attract rain-clouds, even if they existed. In any case, it's unlikely that enough water lies on the surface to allow solid rain-clouds to form through evaporation. Thin mists must certainly occur, but not rain as we know it.'

They moved forward carefully and knelt down at the pool's edge.

The vegetation on Mars, as they knew, consisted mainly of lichen and mosses, pale and dry on account of the paucity of moisture.

Here it was different. There was moss in abundance, but it

grew longer and lusher than the Martian variety, rooted as it was in a damp soil.

The narrow margin of green contained other plants which Dr Hughie thought resembled *Isoetes*, or quillwort. Their narrow, flail-like leaves were either bunched up among the moss or spread out on the surface of the water.

In the cloudy grey pool there was no trace of fish or of other creatures of comparable size; but they saw at once, from little movements and ripples, that it contained life. Clearly, however, it was life of a rudimentary kind, which probably fed on the decaying plants or even, perhaps, on itself: slime moulds and algae so small that only their trails in the water could be seen without difficulty.

Janie uttered a small squeal of surprise as something broke the surface, skimmed it for a fraction of a metre and then disappeared again.

'Possibly an amphipoda,' said Dr Hughie. 'Saladin's version of a freshwater shrimp. It certainly darts about like one.'

He took from his thigh-pocket a wooden box containing a number of labelled phials. With one he scooped up a sample of the water. Into another he put fragments of moss and into yet another a root and leaf of the plant resembling quillwort.

To Malone, Janie and Steve he handed three others, one to each. Fumbling for his scripto pen, he said: 'While I mark the labels on my samples, do your best to scoop up some of the algae. Amphipoda, too, if possible.'

This was easier said than done. The mouths of the phials were small, the tiny forms of life hard to detect in the murky water. But after a few patient moments of trial and lack of success, Steve announced that he had captured part of a swarm of algae, while Janie, kneeling down almost in the pool, declared triumphantly that a miniature shrimp was swimming about in the water which filled her phial.

Malone said: 'I must be ham-fisted. I haven't got a thing as far as I can see.'

'The water in your phial may be thick with bacteria,' Dr

Hughie encouraged him. 'Let's label it "Burke's Bugs Anonymous"!'

The phials were replaced in the box and the box returned to Dr Hughie's pocket. They began to walk again, skirting the pool. Between them and the pillar and the cliff lay the stretch of desert they had seen before landing. From the air, the scattered green markings on its surface had been well defined. From ground level they were more difficult to see.

It was an unusual experience for them, listening to their feet crunching among the sharp grey gravel and sand with which the ground was carpeted. On the Moon, the lack of air caused a lack of sound, because sound waves cannot exist in a vacuum. On Saladin sounds surged in their ears, which, though faint by Earth standards, were yet familiar. It was as if Saladin were a ghost of Earth, with ghost men lurking behind every boulder.

But the experience was rendered unremarkable by an excitement in their bodies which grew with every passing minute.

About half way from the pool to the pillar rock the markings became more apparent. They were made of green sand. It looked finer and more glassy than the usual grey variety, which was coarse and sharp. Some of the grains were stuck together, as if fused by intense heat.

Sprinklings of this sand, like the 'rays' of a starfish, led inwards to a large and thick central deposit. Even at the 'hub' the green in the sand was faint and transparent. It had looked much more brilliant from above.

They glanced towards the pillar, still five hundred metres away. Then, almost with reluctance, they knelt down to examine the coloured sand. Round them a small wind was blowing.

Steve lifted a handful and let it trickle from his glove. 'It reminds me of something,' he said.

Malone looked at him through the perspex of his hood. He did not speak, though it reminded him of something, too.

Dr Hughie bent forward until his face was close to the thickest part of the deposit. He drew in a long breath. He said: 'What do you think, Burke?'

'There must be some other explanation,' replied the coscoxswain. 'It's simply not possible.'

'What's not possible?' said Janie.

Steve exclaimed, with sudden recognition: 'I know what it reminds me of! On my last leave on Earth I went to see the old White Sands testing-ground in New Mexico. It's a kind of outdoor museum now. They showed me the green fused sand that had been created by the first nuclear explosion. It was exactly like this.'

The wind continued to whine in their ears.

Presently Dr Hughie said: 'They once fired a nuclear powered rocket from White Sands. About a hundred and fifty years ago. Close to the pad, after launching, they found the sand fused and coloured green.'

As if arguing with himself, Malone said: 'I can't believe it! The implication is beyond reason!'

'Could a natural nuclear explosion not have happened?' Janie found it an effort to talk with lightness, but the men were beginning to sound too grimly laconic, and she felt it was up to her to restore the balance. 'I mean, haven't I read somewhere that traces of a nuclear explosion have been found in the Middle East: green sand like this, in the Chaldean Desert?'

'Right,' said Malone.

'Well, as far as I can remember, the geological explanation is that it was created when a meteor struck the Earth so violently that it caused a nuclear explosion. Couldn't something like that have happened here?'

'I don't know,' said Malone.

They stood up. They looked down at the sand, then up and away towards the pillar. There was a tightness in their nerves and muscles. They were like wanderers in the dark, on the edge of danger. They were far from Earth, on the surface of a lost, inhospitable planetoid. Nevertheless, they knew now that in some way Earth and Saladin had a relationship, as if one were a complement of the other. They had the feeling that Saladin was familiar, that they had been here before.

'What about taking samples?' said Steve, trying to play along with Janie's assumed practicality. 'Of the green sand, I mean.'

'We can get them on our way back.' Malone squared his shoulders. 'Time we were moving on.'

The preliminaries were over. They were approaching the kernel of the mystery.

'Yes. Let's go,' said Dr Hughie.

Even at fifty metres the pillar towered high. Lava-grey, with a thick base which tapered up into a stem and then bulged out again in a heavy top, it was without doubt a piece of the native basalt.

Their steps quickened. Malone said: 'Could it possibly have assumed this upright position by accident?'

'Part of it – perhaps most of it – is buried deep in the ground,' Janie said. 'You'd almost think . . .'

'At this moment we're end on to it.' Steve had suddenly raised his voice, unaware that he was doing so or that he was interrupting Janie. 'But that rounded base, that symmetrical stem – I could swear they're artificial!'

'And above them there's a kind of lumpiness, like a pattern.' For once Dr Hughie's voice was harsh. As they veered left, almost running, and saw the pillar from the front, he began to shout: 'I was right! I was right! It *is* carved!'

Steve felt himself shaking. There was heat in his body that made him sweat. It had nothing to do with hard physical exercise. His breathing was quick, as if he were labouring in a long race.

Janie gasped: 'Oh, Steve, what is it?'

They stopped, ten metres from the swollen base. They gazed up at a long, blank face, weathered and worn but still recognizable as a face, with hollow eyes staring out across the motionless landscape of Saladin.

'Even through glove and insulated fabric, Malone's grip on Steve's shoulder was vicious. 'Whippy said it,' he muttered, 'and I refused to believe him. It's exactly like an Easter Island statue!'

9 | Palaces of ice

IN the year 2051, man's knowledge of space and of the Moon and the planets was a great wonder even to himself. Every week more exciting discoveries were being made. There was now no mystery about the Moon, or about Mars, Venus, Jupiter and Saturn. Soon there would be no mystery about Saladin, either.

Science was advancing with giant strides.

On Earth, using computers of the utmost sophistication, man had attacked the problem of food distribution, and now starvation and malnutrition were almost unknown. At the turn of the century, all the big oil companies on Earth had been amalgamated into a non-profit-making authority called Universal Petroleum, whose chemists had then evolved a process by which tiny organisms, feeding on the wax content of mineral oil, eventually became almost pure protein. Protein deficiency, from which more than half of the world's population had suffered for centuries, was no longer a problem.

Man had also evolved through radio and television an educational system which offered knowledge to young and old in every corner of the world; and pockets of ignorance, the cause of so many quarrels in the past, were now few and far between. A cure for cancer had been found, and it seemed probable that in the next twenty years a new drug might render the common cold practically extinct, like tuberculosis and the bubonic plague.

On the Moon, the colony produced and processed its own oil and iron ore. The staging post at Aristarchus provided a convenient refuelling point for ships bound for Mars and Venus. Part of the Hospital was a weightless refuge for people gravely ill with heart disease; and in the past decade hundreds of patients had returned from it to Earth, rested and restored to normal vigour after a course of treatment.

Diamonds were plentiful on the lunar surface, the product of carbon crystallization resulting from volcanic activity. At one stage their discovery had caused panic among financiers on Earth. To postpone the speedy crumbling away of their monopolistic fortunes they had employed a Public Relations firm which had almost succeeded in persuading some innocents that Moon diamonds were vastly inferior to the Earth variety. But honest reporting in newspapers and on radio and television had exposed this propaganda as a lie. Like many other forms of advertising which depended on the gullibility of uneducated people for their success, it failed in the end to achieve its purpose and was discontinued. The diamond profiteers retired into oblivion, still exceedingly wealthy but now divested of the power to make themselves rich at the expense of others.

But though diamonds had been plentiful on Earth – and because of a free market as cheap as coal – they remained 'a girl's best friend'. Expensive no longer, they were still beautiful, and beauty had come to be regarded by men – and more especially perhaps by women – as their most prized inheritance.

On a spiritual rather than a physical plane, man had also tackled the problem which had caused him most trouble in the twentieth century: the problem of racial and international suspicion and hatred. The change had come about only gradually, through education and through a general acceptance of the philosophy of the brotherhood of man. Old prejudices still existed, however, close under the surface; and perhaps the greatest threat to progress were certain reactionary individuals, including a few newspaper proprietors, who, mainly in an ᵃᵗ tempt to cling to personal wealth and power, still played on those prejudices by preaching the superiority of one race over another, of one country over its neighbour. Fortunately, however, though people and governments still argued loudly with each other, in general it was with judicial tolerance. The idea of using violence and destruction to achieve an end had become abhorrent to the vast majority of the human race.

Thanks mainly to the example of the Space Commission, which was organized and conducted successfully on an international non-racial basis, man was at last using his moral muscles and stretching out to solve the mysteries of the universe. Many of those still defied solution: the origin of life, for example, and the cause of lasting love between a particular man and a particular woman.

As far as positive results were concerned, the study of extra-sensory perception continued to be disappointing, though within the past year an Egyptian psychologist had been able to communicate, through the medium of thought alone, with a monk in Tibet. Many scientific philosophers were now abandoning their interest in the technical conquest of space and concentrating instead on the subject of thought transference as a possible means of future communication with the inhabitants of distant galaxies. Reactionary groups and individuals, scared by the prospect that one day the contents of their minds might be exposed to the scrutiny of others, did their best to belittle and obstruct the progress of the new science.

Other less important but nevertheless intriguing mysteries also remained unsolved. Some of them concerned man's past rather than his future. The statues on Easter Island were a case in point.

Easter Island is still administered by Chile. Treeless and of volcanic origin, it lies in the Pacific Ocean some 4,000 kilometres west of Valparaiso. Its name derives from the fact that it was discovered by the Dutch Admiral, Jacob Roggeveen, on Easter Day, 1722.

Above the beaches stand rows of huge grey statues hewn out

of single blocks of stone, some almost ten metres high. Rising from platforms of superbly carved masonry, for the most part they represent only a head rising from a long neck. The heads, long and coldly expressionless, are recognizably human; but they resemble no modern type of man.

For centuries, until the extraordinary discoveries were made on Saladin in 2051, archaeologists had been unable to account for their existence. Especially were they puzzled by the out-landish faces portrayed. It had been discovered that the present statues were carved and erected by neolithic seafarers who settled in the island over 3,000 years ago. But it had also been confirmed, following a radiographic study of fragmentary re-mains, that such early settlers had found similar statues already existing on Easter Island, the last traces of a civilization of extraordinary antiquity. Those ancient statues had been broken and in need of repair. The neolithic men, therefore, being ex-pert stone-masons, had created new statues in their stead, after-wards destroying the disintegrating models.

Nothing was certain, however, and the mystery had become even more complicated when wooden tablets were found in some of the island caves: tablets covered by hieroglyphics which until 2051 were completely undecipherable.

This was the background to Malone's tense and even awe-struck mood as he looked up at the blank-eyed face on Saladin and muttered: 'It's exactly like an Easter Island statue!'

Janie put into words what the others were thinking: 'But this means – this means we're not the first people to have landed on Saladin?'

Malone struggled to adjust his mind to the almost incredible truth. He spoke in a voice controlled and matter-of-fact, a voice intended to reassure his companions. 'Looks like it,' he said.

Steve said: 'How long d'you reckon this statue has been standing here?'

Malone shrugged. He couldn't trust himself to sound so matter-of-fact a second time.

It was Dr Hughie, stepping forward to touch the grey stone with his glove, who attempted an answer. 'Without a complete geological survey of Saladin, it's impossible to make an accurate estimate.' He was having trouble with a nerve-twitch in his throat. 'But even in an erosive climate like that of Earth, some of the Pyramids in Egypt are still there after seven thousand years. The carved gateway of the prehistoric city of Tiahuanaco in the South American Altiplano is said to have been erected more than fifty thousand years ago. On Saladin weathering seems to occur much less readily than on Earth.' He coughed, shifting his gaze from the statue to Steve, the expression in his eyes almost apologetic. 'I shouldn't be surprised,' he said, 'if it has been standing here for a thousand centuries.'

Janie drew in her breath.

Steve sighed and said: 'We didn't bring the cameras.' But he said it with an intonation of thankfulness, as if the photographing of this monstrous memorial of a bygone age might have proved an unpleasant chore.

'Cameras will come on the first expedition. Scores of them.' Malone withdrew his attention from the statue. His face and voice were grimly purposeful as he went on: 'There are caves on Easter Island in which ideograph tablets were found. There are caves here, too.'

'The statue is looking straight at them,' said Janie.

Malone nodded. 'I noticed that. In fact it's looking at one particular cave. That big one in the middle.'

At last he was facing up to truth. At one stage in the history of the universe intelligent creatures like themselves had stood on the arid soil of Saladin. Whether they had lived on the planetoid or had merely visited it would soon be decided by scientists from Earth. Meanwhile, what seemed a possibility was that the race of men who had carved the first mysterious monuments on Easter Island, from which the neolithic copies were made, had also carved this statue.

And what was the significance of the green fused sand? Here again a fantastic answer had to be considered: namely, that the men responsible for the statue had also possessed a nuclear-powered space vehicle. This could have landed and then perhaps taken off again in the patch of desert behind them.

Scrappy memories of Moshe Zack's lecture possessed their minds, in particular his reference to the Mohammedan legend of the 'friendly star', according to which the ancient people of Earth had travelled to it on 'wings of light' or in 'chariots of fire'.

Inhibited by years of scientific training and by every law of logic acquired at school and college, they struggled to reject the daunting implications. They were experiencing a nightmare. Soon they would wake up. To the best of his ability, however, Malone tried to persuade himself and the others that they were not asleep.

He said: 'This statue was erected as a landmark to be seen from the air. We saw it. Now it is telling us to go to the middle cave.'

Stiffly he began to walk, heading for the cliff, which was a hundred metres further on. Dr Hughie plodded by his side. Steve and Janie came behind, Janie holding Steve's hand tightly. Steve felt as he had done for a few minutes after an amateur boxing match in New York, when his opponent had knocked him out: dazed, mentally sluggish, ready to accept the most unlikely argument for the sake of peace.

The cliff stretched from horizon to horizon. It was only about thirty metres high, a long regular rift in the otherwise irregular surface of Saladin. But it seemed to soar higher as they approached, staring down at them with timeless impassivity. It reminded Steve of the expressionless face on the statue.

The caves were small fissures at its base. Their openings and inner walls were smooth, which suggested that millions of years ago they had been washed by an ancient sea. On the other hand, the original cracks in the basalt could have been widened and chipped clean by expert stone-masons.

They reached a point about twenty metres from the middle

...saw something above the entrance which made the second possibility seem the more likely.

Nobody spoke. They looked up at the thing in the cliff. The sand, the pillar and now this. It was a logical progression. They were shocked into accepting the evidence of their eyes.

And finally into speech.

Dr Hughie said: 'That inscription is no accident of nature. It was chiselled and hammered out of the stone by men of artistry and skill.'

'And it was meant to last,' said Malone.

Sombrely, Steve added: 'Like the statue, for perhaps a thousand centuries.'

In a small voice Janie said: 'Can anybody tell me what it means?'

Malone shook his head. 'It resembles the Easter Island script. If it *is* the Easter Island script, then *nobody* can tell you what it means. It's so ancient and out of tune with modern thought processes that it has never been deciphered.'

They lingered there, looking up, as if expecting a miracle of revelation. But the series of hieroglyphics remained starkly unreadable. Below them the cave loomed wide and dark, tugging at their minds.

Malone said: 'You have the inspection torch, Steve?'

'Yes.'

'We ought to have a look inside. Lead the way, will you?'

'Sure.'

Steve took the torch from his thigh pocket. As they approached the cave he switched it on. He held it in his right hand, directing the beam into the shadows.

Janie kept hold of his left hand. Malone and Dr Hughie walked on either side of them. The cave was roomy enough to have accommodated a line of eight people advancing abreast.

Their plimsolls crunched and slithered among small stones so smooth and dry that they gave off tiny creaks when pressed down by the weight of human footsteps. There was no other sound.

The walls and roof of the cave were smooth and grey, curving upwards and over like the vault of some ancient cathedral. No slime or lichen adhered to them as in a cave on Earth. No life of any kind was evident in the dry, cold silence. Yet each of the explorers had a feeling they were not alone.

When Janie spoke it was in a whisper: a whisper which rose up and rustled above them like the wing-beats of a bird. 'I'm scared, Steve.'

His hand tightened on hers. 'Nothing to be scared of, Janie.'

'A thousand centuries,' she said. 'The statue and the inscription: they were put there to guide us in. We may be the first living creatures to enter this cave for a thousand centuries.'

By Steve's elbow, Dr Hughie coughed a little as a dust spiral rose and floated in through the aperture in his hood. He said: 'Now I know exactly what Adam was talking about when he mentioned an aura of evil.'

The cave narrowed. It became a tunnel no more than three metres high and three metres wide, curving to the left. No sound, no dust, no weather from outside could reach them here.

Steve walked slightly ahead of the others, though still retaining his grip of Janie's hand. The beam of his torch sprayed the dry rock.

They tramped on, noting only superficially the passing of time. A long curve to the right followed the one to the left. Small eddies of air blew about them. It occurred to them all that ventilation shafts must exist somewhere in the solid rock; but they still refused to admit to each other the logical implication of this.

The tunnel straightened out again, then turned sharply left, and Steve remembered having inspected a tunnel with the same kind of curves and angles at an Engineering Exhibition in New York. It had been constructed to illustrate a new technique for achieving dry storage in damp climates.

Presently the atmosphere grew colder. They found themselves trembling, as if on the point of losing muscular control. The air they breathed had hooks of ice in it which seemed to tear at their throats and lungs.

Then the torch beam moved and failed to find a surface on either side, though the roof was still there, three metres above. Their plimsolls no longer made creaking sounds. They padded lightly on smooth flat stones fitted together like a mosaic.

Steve shuddered. The cold was biting, but his shudder was mental as well as physical. Attached to the lunar hospital was a morgue, in which bodies were kept in a low temperature vault until they could be cremated and their ashes shipped to Earth. This place reminded him of that morgue, with its chill, sad atmosphere.

He kept swinging the beam of his torch until suddenly it glinted on something in front.

Janie said: 'What is it?' The edge to her voice sounded even shriller when it echoed back from the roof.

Steve dragged her forward. Malone and Dr Hughie advanced quickly, moving ahead. Nobody else spoke.

They stopped, two metres away, the light flashing back from glass and metal. Their hearts were thundering. They were still aware of the intense cold, but the blood now rushing through their veins engendered heat which overcame it. What they saw was so awful, in the basic meaning of the word, that the effort to comprehend it was as physically gruelling as a race to the top of a mountain.

They saw seven cylindrical capsules, each about two metres long and a metre in diameter. They were made principally of a dull grey metal but had panels of glass – or what looked like glass – in the tops and sides. Six of them were piled in two columns of three against the inner wall of the rock chamber. The seventh lay in front, at the foot of the piles, alone.

From each capsule a man stared out at them.

The faces were long and expressionless, the open eyes sunken and blank as in the statue outside. The reclining bodies were naked, stretched out and fitted so accurately into the capsules that it was easy to estimate that alive they must have been about two metres tall.

It seemed probable they had lain there for many thousands of years. They must, therefore, surely be dead. And yet as Steve and the others stared back at them, clutching desperately at sanity, they had the feeling that in the capsules animation was only in suspense.

Apparently the capsules were hermetically sealed. Emanating from them was a bitter cold which manifested itself in a slight frosting of the metalwork. But the glass – or whatever the material was – remained crystal clear, as if it had been treated with an anti-frost solution.

The nightmare creeping up on them had now become reality. Janie cowered close to Steve, who put his arm about her. Dr Hughie uttered uncouth words below his breath, which might have been a Nigerian spell against evil.

It was Malone who found his voice. In a throaty gabble he said: 'Do you remember? "And in palaces of ice the mighty ones live on in the heart of the star, safe from terrestrial onslaughts of fire and flood, awaiting resurrection." '

10 | Act first, argue later

THE seventh capsule lay in the morgue, the eyes of the man inside staring out at the cold glazed tiles.

In Benedicts' Row and in the Bachelors' Buttons, in the domes of City Centre and in the School, it was the subject of excited speculation and argument. In the cool quiet of the Library Annexe it was the subject of a Lunar Council meeting, which Dr Akiziwi had been asked to attend.

Twenty-four hours after the return of *Super Nova* with her

extraordinary cargo, Norman the News was still sending stories to Earth. He had had no sleep for two days, but his mind remained alert as with the help of Moshe Zack in Communications he supplied insatiable news editors with detailed information.

In newspapers and on radio and television all over the world, readers, listeners and viewers were being constantly assailed by commentaries and factual analyses. The rescue of Tom Renoir and Adam Dominick and the successful salvage of *Pegasus 5* which was now on the Landing Ground undergoing permanent repairs by expert mechanics, were almost forgotten in the perfervid interest aroused by the discoveries on Saladin.

News of the Earth's reaction to Norman's stories was now beginning to reach the Moon.

As Burke Malone had forecast, the Space Commission was already organizing an expedition due to leave for Saladin within a week. This would give the scientists involved three days in which to carry out their work: after that Saladin would again be moving swiftly out of range of normally fuelled and provisioned space vehicles. Not for another eighty years would an expedition to the planetoid become an economically viable project.

Meanwhile, interim judgments were being issued.

Learned articles by Professor Salvonen were published, describing Saladin's magnetism as being derived from an igneous core surrounded by spiral veins of ferrites, which, reacting to extremes of heat and cold at the planetoid's core and at its surface, set up the magnetic potential. At Saladin's centre the core was probably semi-molten, but at the poles each end of it was thrust above-ground in the form of a batholyth. For the benefit of lay readers, Professor Salvonen described a batholyth as a protruding mass of solid igneous rock.

As for the animal, vegetable and mineral samples brought back to the Moon by members of *Super Nova*'s crew, these had been examined and analysed at once by Professor Lindt and his team in SCO. Within hours an account of their constituent elements – along with pictures in colour – had been relayed by television to scientists in New York, London, Moscow and Tokyo. Now it seemed to be generally agreed that Dr Akiziwi's original assessments of the life existing in and around the pools had been remarkably accurate. WILDFLOWERS AND SAND-HOPPERS FOUND ON MYSTERY PLANETOID had been an early headline in a British newspaper. An American tabloid had featured BURKE'S BUGS ANONYMOUS. None of the minute bacteria captured in the phials had been found harmful to human life. Amongst them, indeed, there had been identified a hitherto unknown species which promised to have a beneficial effect in the treatment of certain circulatory diseases.

But all this had happened before the Lunar Council released news of the green fused sand, the Easter Island statue and the men in the capsules. It was when such information became known on Earth, along with the admission that one of the seven capsules was now on the Moon, that the furore had started.

One school of thought condemned the cos-coxswain's action in removing the capsule from the cave as being not only sacrilege but also scientific lunacy. According to this school's argument, everything should have been left in place pending the arrival of the scientific expedition. For example, what if lethal bugs were conveyed on or in the capsule to the Moon? In such a case Malone ought to be brought to trial as an irresponsible space-craft commander.

Other commentators took the view that Malone had been right to secure as much evidence as possible, as quickly as possible, of what had occurred on Saladin in the shadows of prehistory. Thanks to his efforts, the official expedition would now know exactly what to expect, and as a result their preparations would be all the more efficient. Danger from lethal bugs was only slight, due to the careful decontamination procedures undergone by all those in the space life-boat and in *Pegasus 5* on their return to the Moon.

Journalists and broadcasters seized on the Mohammedan legend referred to in Moshe Zack's lecture. Much to his shy dismay, Moshe found himself in demand for recorded statements to be broadcast all over the world. He hated personal publicity; but Norman the News saw to it that he 'did his duty'.

The suggestion favoured by most writers and speakers was that a hundred thousand years ago a civilization had existed on Earth capable of inventing – and using – atomically-powered space craft. This would account for folk memories of 'chariots of fire' and 'wings of light' and for the startling discovery of green fused sand not only in the Chaldean Desert in Asia Minor but also in a desert on Saladin.

What had happened to wipe out this civilization was a savoury bone to chew at. Had the Moon – or, perhaps an even older satellite – approached so close that tidal waves had surged across the Earth, leaving only dazed and defeated pockets of human life? Or was the Biblical story of the Flood literally true in regard to long, relentless rain which had drowned generations of materially advanced but morally depraved men and women? Had intelligent scientists, more sophisticated than the legendary Noah and warned by their researches of the approach of the flooding, made sure of the survival of some bodies at least by preserving them in air-tight capsules and sending them to Saladin?

It was just as well that those prolific journalists and broadcasters had no inkling of what was going on in the Library Annexe at City Centre on the Moon. Had they been able to overhear Professor Ernst Lindt talking to the Lunar Council their reports of what he had to say might have sounded so wild as to ensure their rejection out of hand by incredulous editors.

Rod Bueno, Burke Malone, U Thong and Dr Akiziwi listened to their colleague with a kind of wonder. As usual, his logic was difficult to counter.

'We have discovered by analysis,' he said, 'that the material used in the construction of the capsule is an alloy of iron and aluminium achieved by a process unknown to modern science. The "glass" panels are of a silica compound, immensely hard and almost unbreakable, similar to but even more durable than the perspex used for the "windows" in modern space craft. Radium tests indicate that the age of the metals analysed is approximately a hundred thousand years.'

Lindt paused, peering at his colleagues through high-powered pebble-glasses. Nobody spoke.

He went on: 'The capsule is hermetically sealed. But, as you are aware, we have been able to carry out an infra-red ray examination of its contents. The body is virtually afloat in a concentration of super-cold nitrogen. There is little or no blood in the veins. Instead, they contain a saline solution containing about twenty-five per cent glycerol – or something which closely resembles glycerol. The result is that the body, including heart, brain and all other organs, is in a state of perfect preservation, as fresh as it was in life.'

Again he paused, blinking. Malone's chin stuck out, and he continued to frown. Whippy's nutmeg face had acquired an expression of distaste. Dr Hughie looked almost apprehensive.

'Go on, Ernst.' As Chairman, Bueno had to sound judicial.

'The evidence,' declared the German, quietly, 'appears to be overwhelming.'

'Evidence of what?' snapped Whippy.

Instead of replying directly, Lindt shrugged narrow shoulders and continued: 'For the past hundred years there has existed in America a body called the Cryonics Society, which includes among its members many famous politicians, scientists, writers, artists and film-stars. Recently its influence has spread to Europe and other parts of the world. The aim of this Society is to ensure that when one of its members dies, his or her body will be frozen and stored away, in the hope that scientists of the future may be able to unfreeze it and bring it back to life. If the member dies of an incurable disease, then there is a chance that by the time he or she is unfrozen a cure will have been found for it.'

Lindt sat forward on his chair, finger jabbing at a roll of

microfilm on the desk beside him. 'Today,' he said, 'I searched the Library here and found this book, *Never say die*. It deals fully with the Cryonics Society and describes the body preservation process which it recommends.'

'Well?' said Bueno.

'After death the blood is drained from the circulatory system and a saline solution pumped into it. This solution contains twenty per cent glycerol. Then the body is packed in ice and later transferred to a steel and aluminium vacuum capsule, in which the air is gradually replaced by super-cold nitrogen inserted under pressure. Finally the capsule is hermetically sealed and stored in an underground vault specially built for the purpose under Times Square in New York.'

Bueno's lean, dark face was intent. 'So your conclusion from the evidence available is that many centuries ago this method of preservation was known on Earth and actually used?'

'Yes. We have proved that the metallic constituents of the capsule in the morgue are a hundred thousand years old. We have also found that this capsule has not been tampered with in any way since the date of its construction.'

His logic was cruel but unassailable.

Malone said, stiffly. 'I almost wish we'd never found it.'

'Me, too!' snarled Whippy. He was angry but at the same time loath to admit the root cause of his anger. 'Death is ugly enough, but the thought of a living death makes me want to throw up.'

'Why?' said Bueno. 'Death is natural and no more ugly than birth. Ugliness exists only in a man's mind.'

Lindt nodded. 'I agree with Rod. From a scientific standpoint the possibility of a living death is anything but ugly. It is exciting!'

Whippy had no logic to fall back on: only instinct. Stubbornly, he said: 'This frozen creature, he's ugly as sin!'

It was Dr Hughie who put into words the question that troubled Malone and Whippy – and Bueno, too, though he kept his uneasiness to himself. The Nigerian was afraid of the answer he might get. He was more afraid, however, of getting no answer at all.

'Ernst,' he said, 'your book, *Never say die,* does it indicate a method of bringing those frozen bodies back to life?'

'It does.'

The words hung in the artificial air. The small sounds issuing from the Equalizer increased the tautness of stretched nerves.

Malone growled: 'This Cryonics Society, it sure thinks of everything!'

'The method itself,' said Lindt, 'is comparatively simple. A slow withdrawal of the nitrogen in the capsule is accompanied by an equally slow increase of temperature. While this is going on the saline solution is gradually drained from the circulatory system and replaced by a massive blood transfusion. The timing, it appears, is the important factor. The Cryonics Society have done several experiments on which they base their meticulously precise instructions.'

The interdome telephone on the desk began to ring.

Bueno stretched forward and lifted the receiver. 'Chairman here.'

'Steve Murray, sir, Communications. A message from New York. The Space Commission currently in session request more close-up television pictures of the capsule. Direct transmission. Message rating, urgent.'

'Thank you, Steve. Arrange this, will you? Andrew Tyrell can direct. Bill Sedibe in charge of cameras.'

'Right, sir.'

The Chairman replaced the receiver. The interruption had caused only a ripple on his deeper thoughts.

He said: 'I know what you'd like to try and do, Ernst.'

Whippy cut in: 'But you ruddy well won't allow him, will you, Rod?'

'I don't know. Ernst may have a case. Anyway, I'm allergic to snap emotional decisions.'

'Burke, why don't you say something?' Whippy's voice contained an unusual pleading note. 'Suffering hell-cats, we can't go tampering with nature!'

Calmly, before Malone could speak, Bueno continued: 'We have been tampering with nature for a long time: ever since man decided to wear a loin-cloth.' He smiled at Whippy, like a headmaster confronted by a rebellious but likeable pupil. 'In my opinion, if you are faced with a moral or scientific problem you don't ignore it. You do your best to work it out and find an answer, no matter what the consequences may be. Man has been given a mind not as a means of achieving self-gratification but so that he may constantly seek the truth.'

There was a small silence.

Then Lindt smiled with one corner of his mouth and said: 'I'm glad you're on my side, Rod. I am not concerned with the moral aspect, but for the sake of science I should like to work on this body. Dr Hughie tells me there is a large stock of blood plasma in the hospital. If he himself will assist me, I am willing to organize and conduct the experiment. Formally, Rod, I request permission from the Council to proceed.'

There it was, laid on the line, the problem that had been worrying them all and which soon must be resolved, one way or another.

Taking a deep breath, Whippy said: 'No! A hundred times no! I will never agree.'

'Why?' said Bueno.

'I can't tell you why, any more than I can tell you why I'm afraid of the dark!'

Malone rubbed his chin, uncertainly. 'Surely a decision like this is not for us to make. The Space Commission ought to be responsible.'

Ignoring him, Lindt turned away and said: 'Hughie, are you willing to help me?'

The doctor's smooth and ordinarily youthful face had grown older and greyer. He said: 'In my profession I am charged with the care of human life. If we decide to go on, it is my duty to help.'

Lindt nodded. 'There is your answer, Whippy. A man with a brain envisaged a rebirth of his body. He trusted in the scientific skills of future generations to bring this about. We have such skills. The man in the capsule lived a thousand centuries ago. Nevertheless, he is another human being like ourselves, born in the same image. We cannot betray his trust.'

'He looks cold and cruel. He looks – different.'

'The expression on his face may be a physical accident, due to the preserving process.' Lindt pointed a finger at Whippy. 'For your information, I calculate that our chances of restoring his vital faculties are in the region of ten to one against. But if we are successful, think of the wisdom and knowledge he may bring to us: the wisdom and knowledge of a previous Earth civilization which before today we never dreamt existed.'

It was the one argument which could have influenced Whippy. His instincts rebelled against the 'resurrection' of a dead human being. But a vein of curiosity – the curiosity that had made him a scientist and brought him to the Moon – was an integral part of his character. He glared at Lindt but made no further effort to maintain a negative attitude.

Bueno glanced at Malone. 'I can see *your* point, Burke: I mean, about referring the matter to the Space Commission. But our colleagues in New York will already be thinking along the same lines as Ernst. They will bring back to Earth one at least of the bodies still on Saladin, and when they do they will certainly bring in the Cryonics Society and allow them to try out their revival techniques. In the meantime, our medical facilities on the Moon are as good as those in any hospital on Earth, and it seems to me that our low pressure wing offers the most favourable environment possible for post-operative treatment. You agree, Hughie?'

'I most certainly do, sir.'

Lindt saw that Malone was impressed. He said, quickly: 'There is another factor, Burke. You know what the Space Commission is like: slow and ponderous. Consider the delay in regard to the Alpha Main extension. If we asked for permission to carry out our experiment, we might have to wait for weeks, even for months, before it was granted.'

He let this argument sink in, then capped it with another which he knew would appeal to the cos-coxswain. 'This could be a triumph for Port Imbrium, Burke. Against all opposition we went ahead by ourselves with the space life-boat project and built *Super Nova*. Why shouldn't we go ahead with this new project as well?'

'You may be right.' The frown began to lift from Malone's face. 'My great-grandfather was a policeman in Cleveland, Ohio. He came from Ireland. His motto was, "Act first, argue later." '

Lindt permitted himself a thin smile. 'Like great-grandfather, like great-grandson. That's one reason why they made you cos-coxswain.'

Whippy was silent. Albeit reluctantly, Dr Hughie was in Lindt's corner. Now Malone's viewpoint had changed. Rod Bueno saw that the German would have his way. He himself favoured the proposition that the cause of truth must be supported at all costs.

Yet his uneasiness persisted. As a boy, in Brasilia, he had gone to church most Sundays with his parents. From those far-off days, and for no obvious reason, the memory of a Biblical quotation now came back to him: '*The wickedness of man was great upon the Earth. Every imagination of the thoughts of his heart was only evil continually.*'

11 | Man alive

THAT evening the party for Tom Renoir and Adam Dominick was held in Recreation. It was a good party, attended by everybody in the colony not on duty at City Centre or working on one of the distant sub-stations.

Medical tests had proved that all those who had been on Saladin were in good health, unaffected by bacteriological or radiation hazards. Consequent relief had turned into gaiety.

In spite of his injured ankle, Long Tom gave his celebrated impersonations of Napoleon and General de Gaulle. Adam tap-danced to swinging music played by Professor Lindt. The Chairman made a speech, congratulating Long Tom and Adam on their escape and the crew of *Super Nova* on the model rescue they had carried out.

Bueno spoke also about the discoveries on Saladin. Until various tests and experiments had been completed by Professor Lindt and Dr Akiziwi on the Moon and by scientists employed by the Space Commission on Earth, he advised the colonists to play it cool. Speculation was dangerous, he reminded them. High expectations could so easily be followed by disappointment.

As the Chairman realized, however, the maintenance of a strictly scientific outlook was against human nature. On the following day rumours began to circulate concerning the result of the Lunar Council meeting. News leaked out that sophisticated medical equipment was being installed in Ward 3 in the low-pressure recovery wing of the Hospital. Excitement simmered up to boiling point.

At 1800 hours B-dome in the Bachelors' Buttons was jam-packed with young people.

Of its four permanent occupants, Lars Sorenson and Nikki Charles were on duty in Communications, assisting Moshe Zack; but the other pair, Steve Murray and Kushi Mohammed, with Janie O'Donnel's assistance, were playing hosts to Long Tom and Adam, Renée Debussy and Boris Ignatieff, Andrew Tyrell and Bill Sedibe – and, inevitably, Norman the News, who for the first time in three days was enjoying a short break from his journalistic labours.

Having noticed on their way to Recreation the collection of small tracked rovers outside the B-dome air-lock, Hans and Elsa Lissner had also called in. With them were Kurt and Hans junior and two other children of similar ages, nine-year-old Nadia Corelli, the daughter of an Italian couple who worked as physicists in SCO, and her small brother Alfredo, aged six.

A micro-tape machine plugged into the Equalizer was dispensing modern orchestral arrangements of classical music, which, during the past few decades, had gradually ousted all but the most advanced jazz from the lunar pop charts. Young folk absorbed in the study of technological problems and, to a lesser extent, in a struggle for survival on the Moon and in space, had no use for drugs which impaired the sharpness of their faculties, whether such drugs were medical or musical.

But on this occasion nobody was paying much attention to swinging Brahms or Mendelssohn. People were standing in groups, talking urgently, while Janie, Steve and Kushi moved about with fresh drinks and trays of cheese flakes.

On one of her tours Janie was captured by Andrew Tyrell, Adam Dominick, Bill Sedibe and Norman the News.

Norman said: 'What goes on? In the Hospital, I mean.'

She smiled. Her dark blue eyes were frank. 'If I knew, medical etiquette would prevent me from telling you, Norman. But I *don't* know. Honest. All I can say is that I'm due to go on special duty at twenty hundred hours – two hours from now.'

'What about that capsule? Still in the morgue?'

'How should I know. I'm only a nurse, remember.'

'I thought you were my cobber.'

'Oh, but I am, Norman darling. You'll observe all the same that I haven't eyes and ears at the back of my head like a leprechaun. But there *is* something that may interest you. This morning, before I went off duty, a large consignment of blood was ordered from the refrigeration unit.'

'Oh, so Ward 3 *is* in use?'

'Maybe.'

'One thing I do know: Professor Lindt and Dr Hughie haven't been seen all day. It's reported they are in conference.'

'Well, Norman, you're the storyteller, not me. Or not I,

should I say, in the presence of the most famous journalist from New York to Port Imbrium?'

'Blarney!' sneered Norman, shooting out his long neck and looking more like a vulture than ever.

But the small joke failed to ease the tension.

Adam said: 'Talking about refrigeration. It's this question of refrigeration that worries me. That capsule was so cold you couldn't touch it without gloves.'

'Nowadays they're considering deep freeze hibernation for astronauts on long time voyages. To Neptune and Pluto, for example.' Bill Sedibe's black forehead was a mass of unnatural puckers. 'But that would only last for a matter of months or years. Not for a thousand centuries.'

Janie said: 'Have some more cheese flakes, Bill. The Chairman said speculation is dangerous. He is right.'

'Man is born to speculate.' Tyrell's voice was as smooth as his carefully brushed blond hair. 'Did you ever hear of the Cryonics Society, Janie?'

'Andrew, dear, I'm so ignorant!'

' *"And yet so beautiful withal."* ' She did indeed look lovely in her short trousered suit of yellow satin; but the cool Englishman's main thoughts were elsewhere.

He said: 'There's a book about the Cryonics Society in the Library. On film. I noticed that Ernst Lindt was reading it yesterday.'

'So?' demanded Norman the News.

Adam and Bill Sedibe became taut and still.

'I had a look at it myself when he returned it. One section deals with resuscitation techniques. The resuscitation of deep-frozen human bodies, I mean.'

Even Norman made no comment. He took a gulp of his drink. He was mentally tired after his long spell of reporting duty. Perhaps this was why he felt daunted by the sudden idea that he might have to cope with yet another dazzling 'scoop'.

Janie's bright personality was clouded, too. She glanced up at the four men, as if seeking friendly comfort. But none of them would meet her eyes. Their group was a bleak island in a sea of chatter.

With a small, helpless gesture she made her escape.

Talking to Renée Debussy and Boris Ignatieff, she began to feel better. Renée's 'crush' on Boris was so obvious – and so obviously human – that a nagging nightmare was partially charmed away. Their excitement was mainly concerned with the connection between the Easter Island statues and an ancient civilization, hitherto unsuspected.

'Pity the stiffs in the capsules are all men,' said Boris, his arm resting carelessly across Renée's slim shoulders. 'I wonder what the ladies were like a thousand centuries ago?'

Renée pouted. 'Judging by the men, they must have looked awful!'

'I expect the men chased them all the same,' said Janie. 'What's the old proverb? *"Beauty is in the eye of the beholder."* '

'One thing,' said Rénee, 'I'm glad Boris doesn't look like that man in the morgue!'

Janie laughed.

Boris's arm tightened. Gallantly he said: 'And I guess his girl-friend wasn't half as beautiful as my Renée.'

Renée's day was made. Janie moved on again, glad that somebody was happy.

Long Tom was ensconced in a chair, with a cushioned stool supporting his injured leg. Standing round about him were the Lissners, the Lissner and Corelli children, and Steve and Kushi. Young Kurt was questioning Long Tom about the wreck of *Pegasus 5*. Long Tom's answers were carefully technical. He respected Kurt's IQ.

As Janie listened, the talk soon became general. The subject of the capsule was touched upon by Kushi, but the presence of the children was an inhibiting factor. Underneath cool references to Easter Island, however, Janie recognized in the other adults the same excitement as was growing within herself.

She looked up and caught Steve's eye.

He came across and drew her aside. 'You look marvellous, Janie. But you're unhappy. I can see it in your eyes.'

'I'm being stupid. I feel scared.'

'Well, so do I. Maybe we're not cut out to be proper scientists like Ernst Lindt.'

'At twenty hundred hours I go on special duty. I'm scared of what I may have to do.'

'I know. You've helped me in so many things, Janie: I wish I could help you now.'

'You *are* helping. Just by talking to me.'

'There's another thing. I hear the chances of the experiment being successful are ten to one against.'

'Sure. That's how to look at it. And even if the worst comes to the worst – well, it could all turn out for the best.'

Steve laughed. 'That's an Irish one!'

'My inheritance from Pop.' She laughed a little, too. 'What I mean is, that man may have been kind and good. His wisdom could help us.'

'That occurred to me, too. Anyway, I suppose we ought not to sidestep the chance of *knowing*.'

She nodded, looking up at him with lips parted and eyes that remained troubled.

Then the children, led by Kurt, surrounded her. They wanted more glucose drinks. For a time the chatter and noise seemed to acquire a kind of happiness.

At 2000 hours Janie went to the Hospital, changed into her white uniform and put on a surgical mask. Her instructions from the Matron were to report to Ward 3 in Recovery. Having manipulated the airtight connecting doors, she was met inside by the nurse from whom she was taking over. This was Mary Goldstein, the wife of Dr Hughie's senior assistant.

Above her mask, Mary's cheeks were pale, her eyes red and haunted.

She said: 'I'm sorry it should have to be you, Janie.'

'Why?'

'I'd be sorry for anybody, in the circumstances. The blood transfusion is still going on but when it has been completed Professor Lindt says you will then have only another few minutes to wait.'

'So – so they're doing the operation?'

'Yes. They began this morning: Professor Lindt and Dr Hughie, themselves alone. It was sixteen hundred hours before I came on duty.'

'Thank you for telling me, Mary.'

Janie parted from her colleague. Silently, in soft slippers, she walked along a shadowed corridor to Ward 3.

The main section of the Hospital had been bright and cheerful, with a friendly atmosphere of bustle. Here it was lonely, lacking even the whisper of a human voice. Nevertheless, in the low pressure conditions, she felt herself relaxing. A nervous sickness began to pass. Her breathing became less hurried.

Ward 3 was a small apartment, usually reserved for urgent heart cases. On the threshold she paused, allowing her eyes to adjust to the dim lighting. She saw Professor Lindt and Dr Hughie, both masked, beside the capsule. This lay on aluminium trestles about one and a half metres off the floor, its upper half propped open. She saw the glint of a blood container. She saw a tube stretching down from it to a bare arm.

The arm belonged to a body in the lower half of the capsule. With the exception of the arm, neck and head, it was covered by a white sheet. Janie had no difficulty in recognizing the bony structure of the face. Eyes once open and staring were now closed. The body was motionless. There was no sound in the ward except a gentle ticking. This came from a piece of complicated medical apparatus behind the capsule.

Ernst Lindt was intent upon a series of dials. He paid no attention to Janie. But Dr Hughie, supervising the blood transfusion unit, turned as she came in and smiled, his teeth showing unnaturally white in the semi-dark.

In a low voice, he said: 'Take over from me, Janie. Just for a minute.'

She nodded, unable to speak. She tried to concentrate on watching the drip of blood from a container that was almost empty. Anything rather than look at what lay in the capsule.

Then she noticed that Dr Hughie was folding back the sheet and fitting the man's chest with a kind of rubber harness to which were attached pieces of bright metal. And suddenly, remembering similar though less complicated operations, she was fully aware of what he and Ernst Lindt had done and were about to do.

In effect, the capsule was being used as a hyperbaric chamber, a piece of equipment found in most hospitals as an aid to recovery from acute myocardial infarction. To begin with, before opening it, they had slowly withdrawn the nitrogen and increased the temperature. After that, they had raised the upper half and carried out a blood transfusion. From the container in use, however, she realized that this had been no ordinary transfusion. The blood had been oxygenated and had contained a peripheral perfusion factor intended to stimulate, first, the cells lining the blood vessels and, second, the peripheral or outlying vein cells. Janie observed an empty labelled bottle and concluded that in this case the peripheral perfusion factor had been a nucleic acid analogue. When the transfusion was complete, they would then close the capsule again, connect it to the apparatus and insert pure oxygen at twice the normal pressure, at the same time stimulating the heart and lungs by means of electrodes.

In a dim, disconnected way she heard Dr Hughie and Ernst Lindt talking together. She caught technical and medical phrases which confirmed her picture of the operation.

Minutes passed. The blood container now held less than a centilitre of blood. She glanced to the right. The men were standing motionless by the side of the capsule, watching the face of the 'patient'.

She, too, turned her head and looked. With eyes now accustomed to the sparse lighting, she saw that the skin on the high cheekbones, which had appeared yellow-tinged through the 'glass' of the capsule, was now faintly pink. Swarthiness remained, but no longer did it seem like the swarthiness of ancient death.

The silence in the ward pressed in on her. She thought of Steve, wishing he could have been there, longing for the buttress of his dour courage. Using all her will-power, she battled against an insidious panic.

Presently in a voice she hoped would sound professional but which emerged instead as a breathless whisper, she said: 'Blood drip negative.'

'Thank you, nurse.'

Dr Hughie glanced at Lindt. The Professor nodded. Both men sighed a little.

Dr Hughie took the bandage and the needle from the well-muscled arm, then applied an adhesive dressing. Janie stepped back into the shadows. She stood beside the portable aluminium cabinet, which, as she knew from previous resuscitation experience, contained such items as enamel basins, sponges, bandages, lotions, disinfectants, thermometers, phials of drugs and syringes. It would be her duty to use or supply any of these, immediately on demand.

'In this case your bits and pieces may not be required,' Dr Hughie told her, as he wheeled aside the blood transfusion stand. 'If they are – well, the techniques recommended by the Cryonics Society will have failed. And so shall we.'

She didn't know what to think. Or to hope.

She heard Lindt say: 'Now, Hughie.'

The doctor closed the capsule, taking care with the seals. Then, with practised speed, his hands moved on the apparatus behind it. Switches clicked. The silence was disturbed by a drone of power.

Through the 'glass' in the capsule lid she saw movement in the body, then a contraction and expansion of the chest harness. The chest began to heave; but she had enough wit left to realize that this was only because of the mechanical aids. The lids covering the eyes were still dead.

The oxygenation process and the artificially-induced heart and lung massage continued. Perspiration was causing her thin uniform to stick to her body. Her legs felt weak. She remembered her first operation as a trainee nurse, in a San Diego hospital. On that occasion her throat muscles had become so constricted that she had almost choked. The quiet words of the surgeon had reached her through a muffled sieve of sound, and she had felt that she must faint. But this was far worse. Her physical reactions were the same; but there was a greater horror.

Lindt said: 'Switch off!'

Her heart thudded. She drew in a long breath and held it.

Dr Hughie stretched up and flicked the switches. The droning died away. He opened the capsule and propped up the lid.

Leaning forward, Lindt loosed off the catch holding the rubber harness together. The harness slipped away from the bare and burly chest.

Janie stared, then expelled her breath almost in a whisper. The chest was moving of its own accord, with a slow, shuddering rhythm.

The mouth sagged open. Lindt took a dentist's mirror from a sterile container and held it close against the yellow teeth. A thin mist appeared on it.

The man in the capsule opened his eyes. He looked at them all with cold appraisal, and Janie put both her hands to her mouth to kill a scream.

But suddenly the expression in his eyes became warm and happy. The sagging mouth grew firm.

The man smiled.

12 | Moluk

AT his own request they called him Moluk. This, he said, was a
phonetic reproduction of the name he had been given by fellow
scientists in a distant age immediately preceding the Flood
Cataclysm. It meant 'Master of Science'.

He was everybody's hero, on Earth, on the Moon, on Alpha
Main and in space-craft far from any base. Every second of
every hour on the first day of his emergence from the Lunar
Hospital his name was heard and his picture appeared on a
television set somewhere.

The Cryonics Society emerged from obscurity and, over-
night, became a household name. Rich people everywhere
clamoured to join it. The entrance fee was raised from a thousand dollars to a hundred thousand. Founder members became
millionaires.

In Port Imbrium, Moluk was an object of awe and wonder.
Always accompanied by Professor Lindt and Dr Hughie, he
talked to the colonists in Recreation, to their children in School,
to patients, doctors and nurses at the Hospital.

Only twelve hours after his resuscitation he had announced
that he was completely fit and well. Not for a moment after
that did he admit to the slightest feeling of discomfort or
exhaustion. His physical condition was checked at regular
intervals and appeared to be perfect. He gave no hint as to what
his age might have been when his body was encapsulated; but
according to twenty-first century medical standards he could
have been about thirty-five.

He slept in Ward 3 in Recovery, with Professor Lindt and

Hughie on call in the adjoining Ward 4; but at other times he moved about the colony, questioning often and answering seldom, his azure blue eyes bright mirrors of the brain behind them.

He ate the same food and enjoyed the same drinks as did the colonists. He had laughed a little at the first vacuum suit he saw. Dr Hughie had caught a suggestion from the alien mind of contempt for a crude piece of equipment; but nothing more had come of it. Moluk had put on the suit and worn it successfully after only a few seconds' tuition.

To the amazement of Lindt, Dr Hughie and Janie, their 'patient' had appeared to speak his first words in English. This was explained at once by the 'patient' himself, and his words became a text for a thousand newspaper articles and broadcast features: 'I only appear to speak, I transmit thoughts. Thoughts being independent of language, it follows that the listener receives them in the language he is accustomed to speak. Similarly I understand what he is saying, because I can read his thoughts.'

The extra-sensory perception students had a field day. Here was a living example of what they had always believed possible – a mind trained to circumvent the barriers of language and distance. They bombarded the Moon with requests for further details of Moluk's methods. But Moluk seemed disinclined to discuss the subject further. Indeed, as far as information was concerned, he was proving more of a 'receiver' than a 'giver'.

To Lindt he said: 'I must first become acquainted with a strange environment and an unfamiliar mode of thought. I must decide on what level of intelligence I can communicate. Afterwards, I may tell certain people many things.'

He spent a great deal of time intensively studying books, microfilms, maps and space charts. But when he relaxed he was charming to everybody.

Some of the girls, like Renée Debussy, thought him ugly. On the other hand, Renée in particular was flattered by his compliments and masculine admiration. When he visited the

Chairman's office in ADMIN he always appeared to be more interested in Bueno's little French secretary than in Bueno himself. She was repelled by his looks, but her mind was stirred by a vision of pleasure and high destiny which he seemed to be offering her.

Young men – Lars Sorenson and Nikki Charles, for example – were astonished by his quick grasp of radio theory and practice. They were also fascinated by a suggestion projected from his mind into theirs that as far as he was concerned mental telepathy made radio unnecessary.

Both Juan Carranza and Boris Ignatieff, along with a few of the younger scientific executives, were his fervent admirers from the start. They envied his cool grasp of every problem presented to him by a civilization far removed in time from the one he had known. They perceived in him – or received from him – a promise of leadership, enlightened and original, a promise of something immensely valuable that he could teach them. With anticipation, even with excitement, they listened and marvelled and waited for his word.

Steve and Janie also felt the attraction of his personality; but like Moshe Zack and Kushi Mohammed they were inclined to reserve judgment about him.

He patted children on the head and with a secret smile conveyed to them the idea that a wonderful future awaited them. They gazed up at him with interest but stayed silent and offered no returning smiles. Andrew Tyrell, instinctively aware of a massive intelligence behind the bright pale eyes, was disappointed by this negative response on the part of pupils under his care. He was wise enough, however, not to make an issue of it.

Rod Bueno, Burke Malone and Whippy were in constant touch with Ernst Lindt and Dr Hughie to receive news of their strange guest's physical and mental well-being. Malone and Whippy were eager to start questioning him on the subject of his previous existence; but Bueno, with characteristic caution, counselled patience.

Like everybody else, the Chairman was conscious of the stranger's superficial charm; but he had a feeling that underlying it all there was a ruthless arrogance.

This feeling, had he but known it, was shared by Hans and Elsa Lissner. As descendants of German Jews, with inherited memories of dictatorial persecution, they were sensitive to the slightest evidence of undemocratic behaviour. Like Bueno, they realized that while Moluk could read the thoughts of modern men – even such as were not expressed in speech – modern men were allowed to receive from him only the thoughts he willed them to receive. The deeper caverns of his mind remained a mystery, and because of this he possessed an advantage which Bueno and the Lissners looked upon with misgiving.

Moluk was more than six feet tall, lean and muscular. The skin of his face was drawn tight over protruding bones. Like his scalp, it was hairless.

He was interested and amused when Lindt produced from his pocket a razor powered by a minute speck of radium. 'We thought beards and body hair unhygienic,' he told the Professor and Dr Hughie. 'At the same time we considered shaving a waste of time. We decided, therefore, to dispense with hair.'

It was only the second occasion on which he had referred directly to the past. As an encouragement to continue, the Nigerian said: 'How did you do that?'

Moluk glanced round at the well-filled tables of the Hospital restaurant, where they had been having a meal on the evening of his second day in Port Imbrium. Projecting on a low key, he said: 'By the use of a simple medicament. I will give you the prescription, Dr Akiziwi, in return for what you have done for me. I understand that on Earth medical secrets can be sold with much profit, so it may help you to become rich.'

The glint in his eye was cynical. Dr Hughie had a feeling of shock, even of revulsion. He said: 'I should like to have the prescription for this medicament. But only to increase my professional knowledge. Commercial firms on Earth may exploit medical secrets. Doctors share them.'

A small frown appeared on Moluk's forehead. Being able to read thoughts, he knew that Dr Hughie was telling the literal truth.

He said: 'That is a peculiar point of view. Tell me, Dr Akiziwi, do you not believe that intelligence should reap a just reward?'

'Not at the expense of others less gifted. In any case, intelligence ought to be its own reward.'

Lindt, that dedicated scientist, had no particular regard for moral philosophy. He said: 'This decision of yours to dispense with hair, did it also apply to women?'

'No.'

'Why?'

'Why, Professor Lindt? Let me explain in simple terms. You and Dr Akiziwi have become accustomed to a chaotic civilization in which I perceive no evidence of enlightened leadership. You have accepted the principle that all men are equal. In the Assembly of your United Nations you allow the vote of a small and backward country to cancel out the vote of a rich and powerful one. This is illogical. Similarly, you have accepted the principle that men and women are equal. This also, from every point of view, is illogical. Men are active; women are passive. They are like the positive and negative poles which produce electricity. In our civilization we recognized this truth. We accepted, of course, that women must be cared for, as potential mothers of healthy children. This is their function. Our women did not expect to share in all the benefits created by men for men.'

'Remarkable!' said Lindt. His eyes loomed large through his glasses, as if he were studying a fascinating new laboratory specimen.

Dr Hughie's reaction was different. Almost harshly he said: 'Our philosophy is based on love. On the proposition that every human being has a right to the love and respect of his neighbours.'

'I find this concept of "love" difficult to appreciate,' replied

Moluk. 'It seems to me it is something the weak have invented to brainwash the strong, and the result is an untidy mess. You have been drugged by slogans. "The meek shall inherit the earth." "Blessed are the poor in spirit." These are two examples of which I have become aware, and doubtless there are many others. No woolly talk of this kind was permitted in our civilization. We bred bodies and brains according to the rules of science, leaving nothing to chance.'

But he was smiling as he spoke, and even Dr Hughie felt there was a grain of justice in his argument. He was persuaded, too, for the time being, that in spite of an alien outlook, Moluk was a man of good will, prepared to be friendly and co-operative.

The following day, on Earth, a special meeting of the United Nations was convened to consider the phenomenon of Moluk and his resuscitation. Official reports from the Lunar Council and the Space Commission were read and discussed.

On account of the short time during which Saladin would be close to Earth and the Moon, various members were anxious to know when exactly the exploratory expedition would be ready to leave and also when Moluk would be brought back to Earth. Up to date the colonists on the Moon had handled the situation well enough. But were those rough and ready lunar pioneers fully equipped, either mentally or physically, to deal with the vast store of wisdom ready to be mined from that ancient brain? What if Moluk should die suddenly on their hands, many of his secrets still unrecorded?

The acting President, a bearded Rumanian, assured the Assembly that the situation was under control. Space Commission rocket ferries would soon be leaving the Florida Pads loaded with personnel and equipment to be assembled on Apha Main and then transferred to a space ship already lying off the station. The departure of this ship – under the command, incidentally, of the experienced Captain Vermeulen – was timed to take place in approximately fifty-four hours. She would convey an expedition to Saladin and collect there not only pictures and samples of the living matter on the planetoid but also two at least of the encapsulated bodies. On her return journey she would call at the Moon and pick up the living miracle that was Moluk. Within about a fortnight Moluk and the others – provided all medical tests were satisfactory and provided the Cryonics Society's techniques proved as successful on Earth as on the Moon – should be available for questioning by representatives of the United Nations.

The Peruvian member brought up another point. Was everything Moluk said being mechanically recorded? The President had to remind him that Moluk's 'talk' was an illusion and that in consequence his thoughts could not possibly be captured on tape.

This answer created uneasiness in the Assembly, and some members expressed anxiety about the kind of influence Moluk's powerfully projected ideas might have on ordinary human minds.

The President replied: 'We are not children to be swayed by honeyed words. From this man we can learn much. Surely we are civilized enough to accept the good he has to offer and reject anything which we may decide is evil or dangerous.'

'All we have got from him so far,' remarked Raymond Argonne, the grizzled, strong-faced member from Canada, 'is a suggestion that the old world was ruled by an elite: men of erudition like himself especially bred for outstanding mental and physical prowess. But women, children and less gifted males, what was *their* condition a thousand centuries ago?'

'Let us have patience,' the President counselled. 'He has promised to talk more freely when the time comes.'

'What worries me,' continued the Canadian, in his forthright way, 'is that much radio, television and newspaper comment seems to be hinting that a reorganization of society on the lines indicated by Moluk might resolve many of our present arguments and that the imposition of law by an enlightened few could achieve sensational progress.'

The President said: 'I believe your worries are unfounded. Democratic values are not so easily debased.'

'I beg to differ.' The Canadian was always a thorn in the silky flesh of the United Nations. 'For the past hundred years our democratic values have been under attack. Powerful commercial interests in every part of the world are continually seeking propaganda material to further their warlike, authoritarian and racist policies. Certain like-minded sections of the press would jump at the chance of establishing this Moluk as a modern prophet, and education is not yet so liberal or so widespread that millions of their readers might not swallow the bait. There is no question that many could easily be led into supporting a new crusade to replace what some call "messy democracy" with the rule of a deliberately planned "intellectual aristocracy".'

A group of members began to shuffle their feet and make derogatory noises. The Canadian smiled, but on the advice of the President he sat down. He had voiced a warning: perhaps this was enough to be going on with.

The South African member rose and said: 'Has it been established that the Easter Island statues and hieroglyphics are in fact modern relics of a lost civilization, of which Moluk appears to be a living representative?'

The President glanced across at the Secretary General, an American of Red Indian stock. The latter stood up, riffling through a pile of papers until he found the one he wanted.

'This theory has not been conclusively established,' he said. 'But as the Chairman of the Lunar Council indicates in his report, all the available evidence tends to confirm it. The inscription above the cave on Saladin has not yet been photographed, and, as you know, the cos-coxswain of *Super Nova* neglected to make an accurate copy of it. Experts, therefore, will not have the chance to study its form and content until the Saladin expedition sends the first television pictures. It appears, however, that Moluk has promised to reveal its meaning to the lunar colonists at an early date.'

The meeting went on to discuss the powers of persuasive thought which the Lunar Council claimed for Moluk. It was something the majority of the members were unable to understand. They were inclined, therefore, to discount its potency.

And its danger.

13 | Flare alarm

ODDLY enough, it was to a gathering of children in the School that Moluk made his most important revelation. This was on the morning of his third day on the Moon.

As he projected news and pictures of an Earth civilization which had existed a hundred thousand years ago, many adults hurried in from other domes to join Andrew Tyrell and his teaching staff in the audience. Amongst them were Rod Bueno and his wife, Burke Malone, Hans and Elsa Lissner, Juan Carranza, Boris Ignatieff, Adam Dominick, Steve Murray and Janie O'Donnel. And of course, Norman the News.

Nobody admitted it, but something had gripped their minds, compelling them to come.

Moluk spoke – or appeared to speak – with rapid clarity. Even children with only an average IQ found him easy to understand. Ideas flowed from his brain into theirs and were absorbed without effort.

'A thousand centuries ago,' he said, 'the Earth was different from what it is today. You call this time the Chellean Period of the Old Stone Age and deduce from fossils and skeletal remains that the people who then lived on Earth were almost subhuman, eating raw flesh, roots and fruit and using primitive flint tools. You are only partly right. Men of this kind did exist. But they existed in highland regions which I find were spared the worst effects of the Flood Cataclysm. Other areas appear to have been inundated and almost completely destroyed. It was in such areas that there flourished a civilization much more advanced than yours.'

His pale eyes gleamed. Children and adults maintained a guarded silence.

He went on: 'Let me give you a lesson in what you might call Chellean geography.

'Your maps indicate a vast, almost empty ocean between South America and New Zealand. In my former life the South Pacific, as you name it, did not exist. There were seaways, certainly; but a huge area of land partly filled the present gap, stretching south from the equator. To the east of this territory were two soaring volcanic mountains, the tips of which still remain above water. You refer to them as Sala-y-Gomez and Rapa Nui or Easter Island.

'During many thousands of years before I was born, in the period following the First Ice Age, the peoples of the Earth increased and prospered: none more so than the inhabitants of Rumelia, which was the name of the former land mass in the South Pacific. The climate of Rumelia was temperate and healthy. In other parts of the Earth it tended to be either extremely hot, or, as in the polar areas, extremely cold. As a result the people of Rumelia grew tall and strong, while other races became, in some instances, frail and burnt black by the sun and, in others, fat and sluggish in heavy, cold-resistant garments.'

Moluk paused, as if to recharge mental batteries, then continued: 'You have a saying, "There were giants in the Earth in those days". This was first used by less favoured races to describe us in Rumelia. We had a capital city called Lemantis. Here there congregated the rich and the famous, the men of learning and the men of action. They ruled the Earth with great wisdom and, because of their benevolence to all mankind, other races gladly paid them tribute in wealth and honour.

'As centuries went by, the great men of Rumelia decided that

the future prosperity and security of the world could be en-
sured only by the creation of a ruling class with outstanding
qualities of brain and body. By a process of selective breeding,
such a class was gradually brought into existence: men who
could store and disseminate knowledge with the rapidity and
accuracy of your computers and who could also receive and
transmit thoughts without the use of the spoken word. Our
practice of telepathy was based on the discovery that a body as-
sociated with a living brain endows the mind with a quality it
could not otherwise possess and that the organic evolution of
the brain is an important factor in the process. Through centuries of time and many generations the art was perfected, but
in the end only the men of the ruling class in Rumelia were able
to practise it.'

Moluk stopped, his forehead creasing. With an air of near
surprise, he said: 'I perceive in the mind of your Director of
Education a query: "Why did the ruling class keep to themselves the secrets of knowledge and telepathy?" The answer is
obvious. In a battle a general reinforces success. When he wins
the battle it is to the advantage of everybody. The whole world
benefited by our learned skills.'

This time Andrew Tyrell expressed another query in words:
'The Stone Age savages of which you reminded us, how did
they benefit?'

'Savages such as those,' replied Moluk, his mood suddenly
irritable, 'were incapable of learning from us. Their mental capacity was inferior, their will to improve their condition non-
existent. Much to our amazement, they appeared to be happy
in their miserable state. They paid us taxes, as was their due,
which helped to make the world easier for others.'

Andrew Tyrell saw that the children – and, indeed, some of
the adults – were becoming restive. They wanted prehistoric
facts, not prehistoric philosophy. He had a vague feeling that
such a philosophy might cause damage to innocent minds; but
he subdued it and apologized for interrupting their guest's flow
of information.

Moluk recovered equanimity. In his expression there appeared a trace of contempt for the Englishman.

He went on: 'Rumelia produced a society in which the arts and sciences could flourish without financial anxiety. Especially the sciences.

'In medicine you appear to have made good progress, though the thinking behind your research is, in my opinion, less logical than was ours. We concentrated on the preservation of *valuable* life rather than of *all* life, and I think we achieved birth control in a more practical manner than you have done. If a man in Rumelia wanted a son or a daughter he had to purchase a licence. Only then could he cohabit with the woman chosen for him on the grounds of genetic suitability.

'On the other hand, your computers, your telephones and radio links are childish toys compared with the machines we employed to capture thoughts and transfer them on electronic wings to whichever corner of the universe we chose.

'Your metallurgical knowledge, too, can only be described as crude on Rumelian standards. We were able to perfect certain toughening processes obviously still unknown to you.'

Urgent questions burgeoned in the minds of some Scientific Executives, including Burke Malone. Before they could be expressed, however, Moluk said, sharply: 'No questions! Not at this time. I may decide eventually to communicate the formulae for such processes to certain individuals. It depends.' What it depended on he made no attempt to explain.

His attitude jarred on the cos-coxswain. But, after all, the man was a stranger and a guest and Malone kept his peace.

Moluk continued: 'Our astronomy was as advanced as yours, and we had begun to realize, as you have, that many of the sound waves from space, washing in on us like waves of the sea, are in fact electronic transmissions from distant intellects, unknown and not yet understood.' He turned his head slowly, cold eyes surveying every individual in the audience. The children were all attention again. Andrew Tyrell was trying hard to conceal his growing dislike of this strange man.

'And then,' said Moluk, 'when the future of mankind seemed as rosy and promising as a summer dawn, a cloud of tragedy appeared on the horizon. Thousands of years before I was born, one of my scientific predecessors discovered that a large comet, hitherto harmless, had been in near-collision with Neptune. Its course had changed. Eventually, following a new orbit, it would approach to within ten thousand miles of Earth and, on account of its gravitational pull, cause in passing a cataclysm of terrible proportions.

'For centuries the scientists kept the secret to themselves. Had ordinary men learnt of the fate in store for them, the happy continent of Rumelia might have been invaded, looted and destroyed as they sought refuge. Generations passed. Only a chosen few inherited the truth.

'Meanwhile, the scientists began investigating space, with a view to finding a temporary refuge somewhere among the planets. Space-craft were built and launched, most of them powered by nuclear rocket engines, and I believe traces of our first experiments are to be found in a place you call the Chaldean Desert in Asia Minor, which we used because it was at a safe distance from Rumelia and only a few ignorant shepherds were liable to be affected by the atomic blast. But as more and more ambitious voyages were made, in ships and vacuum suits far more sophisticated than yours, it became obvious that in the time available no such refuge could be found. The Moon and Mars also came within the comet's sphere of gravitational influence, and on account either of extreme heat or extreme cold the other planets were all uninhabitable.'

A voice piped up from among the children. 'And then you had a bit of luck and discovered Saladin?' Kurt Lissner's face was flushed with excitement.

'Then we discovered Saladin,' agreed Moluk, coldly. That a modern child, born without the slightest regard for genetic principles, should display cleverness appeared to annoy him. His tall, bare forehead creased. 'I said no questions! Sit down and remain quiet,' he ordered.

Kurt and the other children saw that he was disturbed. His look frightened them a little. They sensed that it frightened Mr Tyrell, too, and none of them, therefore, made any further comment.

Moluk went on: 'The planetoid you call Saladin became known to us as Cantorec, or "Rare Visitor". What interested us most was that it would return to the vicinity of Earth some forty of your "years" before the comet came close enough to destroy mankind. We were also aware that when the Cataclysm occurred Cantorec would be safely out of reach at the most distant point of its elliptical orbit.

'It was decided that for the future benefit of the human race a selected seven men should be preserved according to medical practice and immured on this planetoid, where a comfortable human life was impossible but where bodies could be preserved for many centuries. The seven men were chosen on account of their outstanding mental and physical qualities, and it was envisaged that in an age to come, when the survivors of the Cataclysm had multiplied and the Earth again became civilized, those men might be restored to life and become leaders in knowledge and wisdom.'

Filtered light from the green dome glistened on his hairless head. He stared at his listeners. He said: 'As the most notable scientist in Rumelia, I was first to be chosen. They killed me by injecting a bubble of air into an artery in my wrist. This travelled to my heart and stopped it.'

Somewhere a little girl gasped, and Andrew Tyrell knew that only training in lunar discipline had prevented the gasp from becoming a scream.

From the back Juan Carranza said: 'So you personally knew nothing about the Cataclysm?'

'Nothing. Before I died, however, the influence of the approaching comet was beginning to be felt and I could visualize the course of the catastrophe in almost every detail. First, the tides mounting higher in Rumelia and falling back in the polar regions. Then the ice-caps breaking up, followed, as the ice melted, by flooding and by storms of wind and rain as cold currents of air impinged on the warm equatorial atmosphere. Finally, as the comet brushed past, a great girdle tide heaving high and ringing the world, and violent earthquakes and tremors causing some land masses to tilt up and others to sink underneath the sea.'

As he referred to events which had killed millions of his fellow beings, neither his eyes nor his facial expression betrayed emotion.

'And now,' he said, with chilly calm, 'now my study of the geography of the world, and of its abundant folk-tales concerning a Flood in the Chellean period, confirms that my vision was accurate. Rumelia was almost totally destroyed, though, as we foresaw, a few of its inhabitants survived. On Easter Island, though living under conditions of acute privation, they carved statues in memory of their dead ancestors, in the style of our master sculptors.'

Again he paused, as if to recapture mental power.

He continued: 'At Tiahuanaco, above La Paz in Bolivia, the ruins of a small city built by my contemporaries can still be seen. Before the Flood and the volcanic upheavals caused by the approach of the comet, Tiahuanaco was at sea level, and I am told that its harbour, bordered on one side by a strand of sea-shells, can be clearly traced. Today those ruins stand four thousand metres above sea level, the land there having been thrust upwards when other parts of Rumelia subsided. And here again, at Tiahuanaco, I believe that the skill of our master sculptors is evident, especially in the carving which adorns the city gateway.'

He glanced towards Rod Bueno. 'In the mind of the Chairman', he said, 'there is admiration for our sculptors. This is well merited. They served long apprenticeships, learning how to cut and transport heavy slabs of basalt, learning how to use explosives when ordinary drills and chisels were ineffective. The cave of Cantorec – or Saladin – in which our bodies were preserved was originally blasted out by explosives. As you have noted, it was constructed in a special way, with curves and corners and angled airshafts, following a ventilation pattern calculated to suit the climate of the planetoid.'

Impelled by overwhelming curiosity, Boris Ignatieff ventured: 'The statue and the inscription above the cave, they were put there as guides to future astronauts?'

'Yes.' The affirmative came in a bright flicker of thought. It seemed Moluk had no objection to an inquiry posed with suitable reverence.

'Are the Easter Island hieroglyphics the same as those which form the inscription?'

'They are similar. Your philologists, I understand, have been unable to decipher them. This is easy to believe. Your modes of thought are different from what ours were, and the hieroglyphics, as you call them, are in fact ideographs, which convey ideas rather than separate words and letters.'

'Will you explain them to us now?'

'No.' The dark curtain came down again. 'When I reach Earth I will offer an explanation to philological experts. In return I shall expect to be provided with full knowledge concerning every language on Earth.'

Boris gasped. He said: 'Surely one human mind could never receive and record all *that* information?'

'My mind is not like that of a present-day human, which contains a mass of only half-remembered knowledge. It is trained to store, docket and give answers when required.'

Bueno and Malone exchanged glances. Each understood the veiled thought in the mind of the other: *Here is a human computer, without warmth or generosity. He gives a cent. In return he asks for a dollar. It is an idea which must appeal to many.*

In a humble voice, Boris said: 'Can't you even tell us what the Saladin inscription means?'

'It is a quotation from the work of a Rumelian poet,' replied Moluk, as if humouring a feeble mind. 'It means "Small house, great wisdom".'

In his shy way Steve Murray had resolved to keep his feelings to himself and not risk trouble by asking questions. But now, on an impulse, he said: 'What wisdom?'

His voice sounded so harsh and angry that it surprised even himself. Heads turned to look at him. His broad face with its thatch of red hair took on a stubborn look.

Janie caught his arm and held it against her side. Beyond the desk-rows of children, she saw a light in the pale eyes and felt on her mind the clutch of hate. But she had no intention of transferring her allegiance from Steve to Moluk, though she knew this would be the price of relief from hate.

Steve experienced the power of enmity. His body trembled. He had a sudden desire to fall on his knees and beg this man's forgiveness for his brash conduct. But Janie's closeness gave him the courage to remain outwardly calm and dignified.

Moluk glared. When his glare failed to produce a cowering reaction, the knowledge that he was puzzled entered the minds of many in his audience. Bueno was struck by a fleeting thought: *Is Moluk incapable of understanding the resistant strength of love?*

He was about to try and smooth the jagged edges of conflict by asking a question about the design of a Rumelian space-craft, when a bell began to ring stridently in the loudspeaker of the interdome radio.

The mental tension disappeared in a need for action.

There was no panic, because the children knew exactly what lay behind the warning and were well trained in what they had to do.

In the watch-room in SE, the duty observer had spotted a large flare leaping up from the surface of the sun. From this, radiation particles were already flying out to every corner of the universe. The Earth was in no danger, because these radiations were trapped in the surrounding atmosphere; and indeed, over the centuries, countless millions of captured electric particles now formed the outer and inner Van Allen radiation belts. The Moon, however, with only a vestigial atmosphere, was a naked target for such a lethal bombardment. When a solar flare of a certain magnitude occurred, the warning bell was rung. All colonists were then required to don their vacuum suits and proceed in an orderly manner to the nearest shelter. The operation had to be completed within ten minutes, the time it took for the radiation to reach the lunar surface. Should anyone be caught in the open, too far from a shelter to reach it in time, he or she went as soon as possible to the Hospital in Port Imbrium, or to a medical centre in one of the sub-stations, in order to receive an injection of AR 31, the anti-radiation fluid. The alert seldom lasted more than thirty minutes, by which time even a major solar flare had usually died down.

Like the children, Moluk understood at once what was happening. As everybody in the School began to put on their vacuum suits, he quickly stepped into his.

In less than three minutes, Andrew Tyrell led a line of his pupils out through the air-lock hatch and along a firm path on the lunar surface. He stood at the entrance to the shelter, counting the children, while another teacher manipulated the shelter air-lock and ushered them in.

In their wake followed more teachers and all those adults who had assembled in the school to listen to Moluk.

Suddenly he noticed two things. His count of the children was one short. And Moluk was missing.

Then he saw the small suited figure of Kurt Lissner emerge from the School and start along the path.

Through his helmet radio, he said: 'Be quick, Kurt. What delayed you?'

The reply in his receiver had a background of quick, excited breath. 'Moluk asked me to help him with the zippers of his boot-covers. He is just behind me.'

Professor Lindt and Dr Hughie, hurried and anxious, came running back out of the shelter.

Dr Hughie said: 'Where is Moluk? In the rush Ernst thought I was looking after him. I thought Ernst was.'

'It's all right. He and Kurt Lissner are on their way.'

Within the 'porch' of the shelter, the three men stood and watched. Moluk had appeared behind Kurt, loping towards them. He still had a four-minute safety margin, but his purposeful approach made evident that he was in no mood to take chances. Doubtless in his Chellean existence, he had known all about the deadly perils of radiation.

Half way along the path Kurt tripped and fell. Though his vacuum suit and visor were undamaged, the side of his head, protected only by a ribbed join of perspex and rubberized material, struck against a small boulder, and for a second or two he lost consciousness. He lay there, a sprawled and motionless little bundle.

Coming behind him, Moluk's stride was interrupted. But he paused only to swing his lead-soled boot and kick the inconvenient bundle out of the way. Then he continued to lope towards the shelter.

Andrew Tyrell was thankful that both Kurt's parents were already inside and ignorant of what had happened to their son. In his helmet he heard the mutter of Dr Hughie's voice: 'Damn him!' And Lindt's exclamation, uncharacteristically emotional: 'Inhuman brute!'

All three were so shocked by the incident that Moluk was on them before they could move. Dr Hughie and Lindt received an impression of fierce anger that they had deserted him at a time of danger. Next moment he thrust them aside with ramrod arms and disappeared into the shelter.

Then, forestalling the others by only a split second, Tyrell shambled forward. Three minutes were left before the radiation particles could strike; but he did not think of that and would have acted in the same way even though death had been already present He reached Kurt, quickly found that his vacuum suit was intact, lifted him in his arms and came awkwardly back. As he reached the shelter he was guided in by Lindt and Dr Hughie at the air-lock controls.

Kurt's eyes behind the visor slowly opened. Tyrell smiled down at the boy. The boy smiled back.

'I was frightened,' said Kurt on his radio. 'I moved too fast and lost my balance. I am sorry.'

'No harm done.' With difficulty the Englishman kept control of himself. 'But why were you frightened?'

'While I was doing Moluk's boots one of the zippers got stuck. I looked up and saw his eyes. I – I knew he hated me.'

'Your imagination is too vivid, Kurt. Feeling better now?'

'Yes.'

'Then down you get.' They walked together, with Lindt and Dr Hughie behind them, into the main compartment.

In the balmy air of the shelter they removed their helmets. Most of the others had done the same. Already, in a far corner, Moluk was surrounded by an eager group of adults. It included, amongst others, Juan Carranza, Boris Ignatieff, Adam Dominick and Norman the News.

Kurt moved away to join his schoolmates, and to enjoy a glucose drink as an aid to recovery. Tyrell, Lindt and Dr Hughie caught the drift of Moluk's thoughts and moved close to the listening group.

Moluk was saying: 'My knowledge will cause a bloodless revolution. Those of you who have agreed to work for me will enjoy unlimited power. Be ready to leave tomorrow.'

He smiled at them. It was like a benison. Boris, for one, became flushed with excitement and pleasure.

14 | Law of the jungle

'HE said he is leaving tomorrow, presumably for Earth. How does he propose to do it?'

The flare alarm had long since passed. Now, at 1800 hours, a meeting of the four-man Lunar Council had begun in the Library Annexe. It was Lindt who posed the question.

Bueno said: '*Pegasus 5* will then be fully repaired and ready for flight.'

'And Moluk knows about it?' said Whippy.

'He knows about everything. At this moment, unless his mind is otherwise engaged, he may be tuned in to what we are saying. In any case, I understand Adam Dominick told him.'

Troubled and unhappy, Malone said: 'Do you mean to let him go, Rod?'

'I have been ordered to let him go. By the Space Commission. When they heard that *Pegasus 5* would soon be serviceable they decided to kill two birds with one stone. They want the scout-ship crew for interrogation regarding their forced landing on Saladin. They want Moluk, in order to get from him as soon as possible the secrets of Rumelian science. If he goes in *Pegasus 5* he will be on Earth almost a week earlier than if he waited for the Saladin expedition to pick him up on their return journey.'

Whippy made a snarling noise. 'They'll be lucky if they get any secrets out of that cold, cruel fish! Secrets of value, I mean. Except in exchange for a pile of ruddy dough!'

'If the hints he has already dropped are any indication,' said Lindt, 'the information he has to give could be of immense value to the world. His knowledge of telepathy. His knowledge of metallurgy. His knowledge of space techniques. All stored in the computer that is his brain, ready for instant dissemination. With his help, a hundred years of scientific research might be compressed into one.'

'And his price?' said Malone.

'That is what worries me.' Long dark lines furrowed the Chairman's cheeks. 'What is happening here on the Moon could be repeated on Earth, with tragic results.'

'Get rid of the stinking child-kicker!' exclaimed Whippy. 'Those tycoons in America and Europe who want him so badly, let them have him. And the best of celestial luck to the whole howling hatch of them!'

'I wish it were all so simple. You're working eighteen hours a day in Communications, Whippy, thanks to Saladin and Moluk. You're out of touch.'

'Out of touch? How?'

'Moluk is impressing his will and personality on some of the colonists. I have had unpleasant interviews with both Juan Carranza and Boris Ignatieff, and Burke warns me that later this evening I may be approached by several young men in SE. Carranza and Ignatieff are determined to leave with him in *Pegasus 5*. The others want to resign and travel to Earth in the next available liner. To become his "disciples", they say.'

'Because he's promised to make them rich?'

'Partly because of that. And partly, I think, because of a genuine urge to better the world's condition. The bait of unlimited fresh knowledge is often as tempting as that of money. Trouble is, they're all blind to the consequences.'

Lindt and Malone leant forward, eyes anxious but intent. They were both strong characters, both experts in their particular fields; but when questions arose of philosophy or sociology, they were glad to accept Bueno's initial guidance.

The Chairman continued: 'This evening I had a personal message from my old friend Raymond Argonne, the Canadian representative in the United Nations. You decoded it, Whippy, so you know roughly what it is all about.

'Raymond tells me that wealthy corporations in America and Europe are bidding savagely for Moluk's services and for the services of the six others still on Saladin. They have money and influence. Propagandists are already working in subtle ways, describing them as benefactors of mankind, eager to process and present to the world the technological secrets of Rumelia. The doubts of workers are being stifled by promises of huge wage packets to come.

'Certain newspaper interests are backing up those corporations, mainly for political reasons. It is not being said in so many words, but the whole trend of the editorial argument is that the world has grown too soft. Too much money is being spent in helping those who don't seem able to help themselves:

the unemployed; the old and the sick; the uneducated, both white and coloured; the retarded children; the poets and the artists and the makers of music. Let riches come to those who work for it. Let harsh competition win the day, and the devil take the hindmost.

'This was the climate of opinion in Rumelia. If Moluk is allowed to go his way, unhindered, this is what Raymond Argonne and others – including myself – are afraid may become the climate of opinion on Earth. In the past hundred years, laboriously, we have achieved some co-operation between nations and races. We have begun to see at the end of a long tunnel a society built securely upon the rules of love and compassion. Moluk and his "disciples", by applying the ruthless law of self-interest, will close the tunnel again.'

For some time, in the Library Annexe, there was silence.

Malone was remembering his grandfather's tales of life in America when vice-peddling gangsters ruled the cities with guns, when Negroes were hunted and even killed by the Ku Klux Klan, when a new 'religious' cult could attract millions of uneducated and unhappy paying members and reward its promoters with a fortune.

Lindt was remembering the tales of his ancestors who had lived in twentieth-century Germany. At that time, seeking expanding trade, European armaments firms had stirred up in the space of only thirty years two bloody wars in which millions had died. As the architect of the second war they had chosen a man of no compassion who murdered countless Jews because their humble piety and family affection threatened to block his purpose.

Whippy was remembering the tales told by old Burmese men and women he had known in his youth: tales of British cruelty in India, of Japanese cruelty in Burma, of French, American and Chinese cruelty in Vietnam. Such cruelty, at the time, had been described as necessary to procure peace and 'civilized values'. But in themselves such acts had been uncivilized, and only the perspective of history, enlightened and free from propaganda, had revealed the callous selfishness behind them.

Bueno was thinking about former dictatorships, in France, Spain, Germany and Russia – and, more recently, in his own country of Brazil. Those who were failures in body and spirit, those whose qualities of mind rendered them useless – and perhaps dangerous – to the ruling classes, all had been thrust aside to starve or die, while the leaders collected about them even more wealth and comfort. As far as he could understand, the continent of Rumelia had harboured a similar dictatorship, though Moluk's description had romanticized and even en-nobled it. Of late, greed had been controlled by the power of liberal ideas. Now, if Moluk had his way, Bueno saw with pain-ful clarity that greed would be unleashed again to wreak new havoc in the souls of men.

'Rod,' said Malone, at last, 'yours is a true bill, I reckon. How are we going to deal with it?'

'That is what we are here to discuss. Raymond Argonne pleads with us to prevent Moluk reaching the Earth. For his part he promises to try and stall the sending of the expedition to Saladin, until such time as the planetoid spins away on its remote orbit and it has become too late to pick up the other six capsules. He has support, it seems, from a number of the smal-ler nations.'

He paused, drumming brown sinewy fingers on the desk-top.

He turned to Whippy. 'This is the situation. I should like your views on it. And those of Burke and Ernst.'

For once, Whippy could utter no immediate reply. Malone shook his head and looked sad, like a dog puzzled by human conduct.

Lindt took off his glasses and used a thin paper handkerchief as a polisher. Then, replacing them on his nose, he said: 'We set ourselves up as judges. On the one hand we admit that the material knowledge Moluk has to offer could benefit the human race. On the other, we concede that his philosophy is corrupt and might cause human strife and bitterness. Now we weigh one conclusion against the other and give our decision. Am I right?'

'Right.'

'And if I understood you, Rod, you believe that the world might be better without Moluk?'

'I think so.'

'I am inclined to agree with you. But are we justified in acting upon such a decision? Who are we to sit in judgment?'

'I have put this argument to myself. It has been the cause of my inaction while Moluk influences people like Carranza, Ignatieff and Adam Dominick. It has prevented me from pointing out to him his crime in treating young Kurt Lissner as he did this morning. But now, justified or not, Ernst, I feel we must do something – if only to spare others from the effects of his arrogance.'

After a small hesitation, Lindt nodded. His logic was blurred by a mist of human anxiety.

To Malone and Whippy, Bueno said: 'There is one other development I must ask you to consider. Ernst tells me that this afternoon Moluk announced to him privately that he wishes, as soon as possible, to father a son, in case anything unexpected should occur to shorten his own life. He has been favourably impressed, it seems, by the health and beauty of Renée Debussy. He plans to take her with him to Earth.'

It was as if the two men had each received a body blow. They sucked in breath, then carefully exhaled it.

Guarding his words, the cos-coxswain said: 'Does Renée know about this?'

'Not yet. But her boy-frind does, Boris Ignatieff. He has told Moluk that he is proud for her.'

With unusual economy, Whippy said: 'You are right, Mr Chairman. Something must be done to discipline this man.'

Lindt took out his handkerchief and again began polishing his glasses. He said: 'What can we do, Rod?'

'I suggest we have him in before us, here and now. I will talk to him, explain our code of conduct, try to reason with him.'

'And if that fails?' Malone was glowering.

'We are a free society on the Moon. We have never required a policeman, because everybody recognizes that the safety and well-being of the colony depend on individual good behaviour. But in this case, if argument fails, I am prepared to use force.'

'Right!' Malone thumped his fist on the desk and rose. 'I will go and bring him –'

He stopped in mid-sentence as the door leading in from the Library was thrust open. Moluk stood there, wearing the white linen jacket and shorts supplied to him by ADMIN. By his side was Dr Hughie, grey faced. Behind him were Juan Carranza, Boris Ignatieff and Adam Dominick. Their eyes were bright and threatening.

'I couldn't stop them,' Dr Hughie said.

Moluk advanced to the desk.

He projected a steel-cold statement: 'I became aware that you wished to talk to me. Courteously, I have come, though I know already what your Chairman intends to say.'

Bueno controlled his muscles and remained still, though his pulse beat faster. 'Then there is no need for me to say it,' he replied.

'None. I will remain a free agent. Tomorrow, when the repairs to *Pegasus 5* are complete, Adam Dominick will take command. Thomas Renoir, being injured and therefore unimportant, will be left behind. Dominick will take as passengers myself, Carranza and Ignatieff, and the woman I have chosen.'

'*Pegasus 5* is constructed to carry two people only.'

'I have studied the logistics. There is room for five: myself and Dominick in the pilots' seats, Carranza and Ignatieff on the deck immediately behind us, the woman in the cargo compartment. The weight factor is no problem. There is a wide margin of lifting and braking power.'

'I refuse permission for take-off.'

Carranza, Ignatieff and Dominick stepped forward, faces hard and angry. They were about to speak, but Moluk restrained them.

He said: 'Then I am afraid we must take off without your permission.'

'Has Renée agreed to go with you – "the woman", as you call her?'

'No But she will come.'

'I intend to make sure she doesn't.'

'How?'

Malone had been standing stiff against the desk. Now he took a quick step around it, his face hard, fists clenched. 'I'll tell you how, you beast –'

Quickly the young men interposed themselves between him and Moluk.

Carranza said: 'Don't try anything, Burke!'

Dr Hughie moved forward as if wanting to say something. Ignatieff pushed him back. He stumbled and fell against the hard edge of an aluminium chair, hurting his arm.

The Russian said: 'Crawl in your kennel, nigger!'

Bueno felt cold and tired. So it had happened: by injecting into their minds a continuous stream of poisoned thoughts, Moluk had captured unconditionally the allegiance of these three young men – and probably that of others in the colony. In ordinary circumstances, Carranza, Ignatieff and Adam Dominick were pleasant characters, full of human warmth and affection. But they came from countries formerly conditioned to dictatorship and for this reason had proved more susceptible than others to the offer of 'divine' leadership. Almost imperceptibly, warmth had been forced out of them by callous ambition. It had happened like this before, in the days of Hitler and Stalin. Unless he – and others – could find a means of prevention it could happen again, not only on the Moon but also on Earth.

He raised a hand in caution to Malone and Dr Hughie.

'Wait!' he counselled. Then, to Moluk – 'Let me be specific,' he said. 'You have employed your mental genius to brainwash these men. You are brainwashing others. But I promise you this, we in Port Imbrium will never allow you to succeed in your intention. When you go to Earth – if you ever do go – you will be taken there alone, as a guest under discipline.'

A thin smile stretched the skin on the bones of the man's face. 'How,' he said, 'are you going to arrange that?'

'I am putting you under arrest – you, Carranza, Ignatieff and Dominick. Now!'

He rose. He put out a hand to take Moluk's wrist. Malone, Lindt, Whippy and Dr Hughie were about to lay hands on the others.

With a glimpse of former comradeship, Carranza exclaimed: 'Don't be crazy, Burke! You haven't a chance against us.'

And Dominick appealed urgently to his countryman, Dr Hughie: 'It's all settled, man! If you use force it will be met by force. You may get killed!'

But the Chairman would have persisted in his plan had not angry sounds suddenly occurred beyond the door. Bueno and his friends let their hands drop and stood motionless.

A dozen young men came crowding through the Library into the Annexe. They were all from SE, nominally employed by Malone.

The cos-coxswain faced them: 'What are you doing here? You should be at your work!'

They gave no sign that they heard him. Their faces were blank, unmoved. In a subtle way they had begun to resemble the Easter Island statues.

Moluk said: 'They are here because I sent for them. I did so by telepathy, in order to demonstrate that it is physically impossible for you to arrest me. At this moment we outnumber you more than three to one. If you insist on acting stupidly we will kill you. This could lead to further bloodshed in the colony, all to no purpose. Nothing can stop me leaving for the Earth tomorrow. I perceive in your mind, Bueno, that you have weighed the possibilities and admit my argument is valid. You are determined to avoid strife and death in Port Imbrium.'

Bueno made no answer.

But Malone lowered his head, lunged forward and caught Carranza by the lapels of his jacket. 'You goddamned idiot! You are my second-in-command in SE. Tell these men to get back –'

Moluk flashed quick thoughts. Ignatieff and Dominick, helped by two of the young scientific executives, caught the cos-coxswain, pulled him off Carranza and held him back, twisting his arms until he uttered a groan of pain.

Lindt and Whippy, used only to dealing in words, were shocked and silenced by the brutal action. It was a situation with which they were completely unfamiliar. They felt angry and frustrated that for once their scientific knowledge was useless. The temptation to take the easy course and let Moluk have his way was almost overwhelming. But they suspected an attack on their minds by his personality and struggled to resist it.

Bueno said, sharply: 'Let him go, please. He won't use violence again.'

They let him go. Malone stood rubbing his wrists, glaring as inimically at the Chairman as at those who had hurt him. He found it difficult to understand Bueno's apparently easy surrender.

But Moluk understood. He said: 'Despite appearances, I know you have not given in. You still hope to curb me. Vague ideas concerning drugs are stirring in your mind. They could be mixed with my food and drink or injected into my veins while I am asleep, so that I might become submissive and pliable to your will. Let me explain. From now on until I leave I intend to dispense with the company of Lindt and Akiziwi. I will be guarded day and night by these young men you see around me, according to a duty roster. On Earth I will be guarded by Carranza, Ignatieff and Dominick, all of whom I will reward for their loyalty. Remember, I am at an advantage. Invariably I receive a mental warning of danger, as I did a few minutes ago, and can therefore prepare to meet it.'

A cold, unarguable statement of fact. All eyes were directed towards Bueno.

Even in defeat, the Chairman kept his dignity. Ignoring Moluk, he turned to the others: 'Listen to me – Carranza, Ignatieff, Dominick, all you young men from SE. Can't you understand the consequences of what you are doing? You have been promised a future of prosperity and power. It is a future of slavery, with this man as your slave-master. You and the working people on Earth may become rich, but in order to do so you will lose your individual wills, your individual souls. Human affection is unknown to him. When he has achieved his purpose and no longer needs you he will kick you aside as he kicked young Kurt Lissner aside this morning. Can't you understand all this?'

Dr Hughie ignored the pain in his arm and spoke directly to Dominick. 'You heard him, Adam. You heard Ignatieff call me "nigger". At this moment they are glad to have you as an ally because you are a pilot. But on Earth, when your usefulness is past, they may start calling you "nigger" too. This is the law of our forefathers, the jungle law of divide and conquer. Take my word for it, before it is too late!'

For a second Dominick's eyes showed interest and warmth. Then his mind was subjected to a lash of mental energy. After only a second's hesitation he stepped forward and struck Dr Hughie across the mouth with the back of his hand.

Malone had had enough. His mind was besieged by the weight of Moluk's thought, and he was afraid that he might give in to it. He was like a bull teased and tormented by a toreador. His ancestors in America had all been men of courage, reacting to evil in the only way they knew. He reacted in the same way now.

He hit out at Dominick, his fist catching the Nigerian on the chin and sending him staggering back into the arms of the young executives. With a roar of anger he turned and charged at Carranza. He caught him by the throat, shook him and hurled him against Ignatieff.

In a struggling group all three crashed to the nylon-carpeted floor.

At the back of Malone's mind was the idea that he might get through to the Library and telephone for assistance. It had no chance of success. He was hauled off Carranza and Ignatieff, yanked to his feet and pounded by the fists of half-a-dozen men. They flung him into a corner, and a kick on the side of his head blanked out the pain. Lindt and Dr Hughie knelt to assist him.

The brown in Whippy's cheeks had become pasty yellow. On the desk was a steel ruler, the only weapon he could see. He snatched it up and was about to make a blind attack when Bueno caught his arm.

'No dice, Whippy. Try to play it cool.'

He took the ruler from him and replaced it on the desk.

Moluk said: 'You are dangerous, Bueno. You and your colleagues are all determined to dam the flood of our new knowledge. You are reactionaries and must be treated as such.'

His thoughts were like whips on sluggish spinning-tops, lashing his allies into action. They pulled off Bueno's jacket and tore it into strips and tied his feet and hands with them. They did the same with Whippy, Lindt and Dr Hughie. As Malone regained consciousness they tied him up as well.

Moluk said: 'You will be kept here until I and my aides are launched for Earth. Four of my men will keep watch, wearing vacuum suits. Two in the Library, two here in the Annexe. If you try to escape or to communicate in any way with other colonists, they will throw the deflation switches. The dome will collapse about you, killing you and every other colonist in the Library and in the Recreation Hall.'

Bueno lay half-naked on the floor, looking exhausted and ill. But he spoke with authority to Carranza, Ignatieff and Dominick.

'You see what happens in Moluk's world. Violence in

place of cool argument. Hate in place of love. Use your own minds and think! Counter his thoughts –'

Moluk kicked him in the face.

Presently they were alone in the Annexe, helpless and tongue-tied with shame.

The door opened. Two men came in, wearing vacuum suits and carrying helmets. They sat by the desk. One of them held in his gloved hand a stud-operated extension to the deflation switches.

15 | Death on Piazzi Smyth

RAYMOND ARGONNE stood up in the Assembly of the United Nations. He spoke for an hour. He had the baldness, the haggard good looks and the clear, hard voice of an old actor.

He described the message that had come to him from Norman Grant in the Moon. It had been radioed through at 1920 hours that evening, while Moluk and his 'disciples' were otherwise engaged in the Library Annexe and could not, therefore, interfere with it. The gist of the message was that Moluk was 'taking over' on the Moon and that his journey to Earth the following day, if allowed to happen as planned, might prove a calamity for the world.

Argonne said: 'At nineteen-thirty hours the message was cut short. Grant's last words were these: "Carranza and Ignatieff have entered Communications. For the time being Moshe Zack, Steve Murray and I must appear to play along with them. All I can say is, *beware of Moluk*."

'Since that moment,' continued the Canadian, 'the lunar radio has been silent. The Space Commission has been calling Port Imbrium minute by minute. There is no reply.'

He paused, then made his peroration: 'Tomorrow, the Saladin expedition is scheduled to leave Alpha Main. I beg of you, my friends, let us divert it to the Moon. Bueno and his Council are in need of help. Even if such a diversion means that the expedition cannot now reach Saladin, that the secrets of this strange planetoid may not become fully known for another eighty years, what does it matter? It may be, indeed, that on Earth we are not yet ready to cope with what Moluk represents. Have you seen the ticker-tapes this evening? Prices of certain stocks are booming on the exchanges from New York to Tokyo. The savage law of materialism is about to prevail. A century of human idealism may be dissipated like a cloud of spatial dust. But if we speak now with a united and decisive voice we can still defeat self-interest, we can still rescue the idealism for which we have worked and prayed.'

He slumped down in his seat, wiping his domed forehead with a handkerchief. He knew he had been talking what he himself might have described as 'a load of old corn'; but at least the thoughts and aspirations behind the banal words had been sincere. His fellow members accorded him an ovation. Even the translators in their glass boxes joined in the applause.

That night an order was received by the Space Commission to divert their Saladin expedition to the Moon. Big commercial corporations and their supporting newspapers screamed with disappointment. They still hoped, however, that Moluk would soon become available to them, and though prices fell on many stock exchanges, the falls were only fractional.

Argonne knew that he had accomplished his part of the bargain: no capsules from Saladin would be brought to Earth – not in his lifetime. Now it was the responsibility of Bueno and his colonists to deal with Moluk. But hourly as the radio link stayed silent, he grew more and more afraid that the rescue expedition might reach the Moon too late.

For the first time in history, the colonists were sharply divided, one against the other.

There were those whose minds had been taken over, who could see no danger in allowing Moluk freedom of action and who argued that the benefits he could bestow on society far outweighed any harm he might do. There were others, more mentally stable perhaps or considered of such unimportance by Moluk that he could ignore them, whose minds were still their own and who tried unsuccessfully to appeal to the loyalty and affection of old friends. Moluk, they said, must be put under some kind of restraint or he might destroy the whole laboriously-built edifice of human tolerance and good will.

But nobody *did* anything to support their arguments. They were waiting for Bueno to give them a lead.

Steve Murray, Moshe Zack and Norman the News, together in the green-tinted silence of Communications, were becoming worried about the absence of their Chief, U Thong.

Late the previous night, soon after Norman had sent his message to Raymond Argonne in New York, a telephone call for Steve had come from the Chairman. For the time being, until Moluk should take off in *Pegasus 5* the following day, Communications was to be closed down except for internal calls. The United Nations, Bueno said, were trying to decide what should be done about Moluk, and he was concerned to spare Port Imbrium an unsolicited spate of advice. Meanwhile, the Lunar Council would remain in session, analysing certain information being supplied by Moluk, and there must be no attempt to get in touch with them in the Library Annexe.

At the time this had seemed a reasonable arrangement, because Earth interference in lunar affairs had often irritated the colonists, and the man Moluk was a phenomenon whose future had to be carefully considered. But now, at 1100 hours the next morning, with *Pegasus 5* already on the Landing Ground and due to leave at midday, Steve, Moshe and Norman were beginning to wonder if Bueno had telephoned his orders under some kind of threat. His voice, Steve remembered, had sounded strained and tired.

Throughout the night and during the morning Moluk and his three principal lieutenants, Carranza, Ignatieff and Dominick, had behaved correctly and with due regard for everybody's feel-

ings. But now they were ordering people to stay away from
Pegasus 5 on the Landing Ground, and an atmosphere of tension was building up under the domes. Why had there been no
further news from the Chairman? Why was the telephone to
the Library apparently out of order? Why had Steve, visiting
the Library to try and find the fault, been politely but firmly
turned away by two young executives from SE, who said they
were carrying out orders from Burke Malone?

Internal calls were few. At 1115 hours Steve and Norman
left Moshe to deal with them alone and went to Recreation.
The place was full of people drinking coffee and talking in
edgy voices. Faces were pale and tense. It seemed that little
work was being done that morning in Port Imbrium.

Steve and Norman found Tom Renoir in his usual chair
talking grimly to Hans Lissner and Kushi Mohammed.

As they came in, removing their helmets, Tom said: 'Have
you heard?' Not even waiting for a response, he hurried on:
'They're taking Renée. Moluk is taking Renée, as his
"woman"!'

Even Norman was struck silent. Then he said, quickly: 'Who
told you?'

'Adam came in a minute ago to bid me good-bye. He said
that only three people knew – Moluk, Boris Ignatieff and Ernst
Lindt. Renée herself had not been told. But now, he explained
to me, there was no point in keeping it a secret, because Ignatieff has already brought her to the scout ship.'

'Did she go of her own free will?' asked Steve.

'I put the same question to Adam. He said the problem
didn't arise. She wasn't told *why* she had to embark in *Pegasus
5*. Ignatieff simply conveyed an order from her boss, the Chairman.'

Hans Lissner said: 'There is something wrong. Rod Bueno
would never issue such an order without consulting Renée
first.'

'Something is horribly wrong.' Tom used both his hands to
change the position of his injured leg on its stool. 'Adam is not

the sensitive character who was my friend. He has become hard. His eyes show no feeling.'

Hans nodded. 'Juan and Boris are the same. I put it down at first to their intense interest in what Moluk might be able to teach them. I was interested myself. But now I see another side to it. They condoned Moluk's treatment of Kurt. Now they condone his scheme to take Renée Debussy with him to Earth. Apparently even Boris, who was Renée's boy-friend, approves of it. They have become cold and inhuman, and Juan and Boris were never cold and inhuman before.'

Steve looked up at the clock. '*Pegasus 5* will be gone in less than thirty minutes. The Chairman knows the Earth doesn't want Moluk. Why isn't he doing something about it?'

In his precise way, Kushi said: 'We have been told that the Chairman is in conference with Burke Malone, Ernst Lindt, Whippy and Dr Hughie.' He glanced towards the Library door. 'In there,' he added, 'in the Annexe. But as you yourself have discovered, Steve, no one is being allowed into the Library. Are they really in conference? Or are they prisoners, with those SE fellows acting as warders?'

'That,' said Steve, 'is what we ought to find out.'

'Too right, cobber!' said Norman.

With Hans and Kushi they began striding towards the Library.

'Stop!'

Moluk stood inside the air-lock with Juan Carranza. Both wore space-suits and were carrying helmets. The muted voices in Recreation became abruptly still.

Steve and his friends experienced an assault on their minds. They obeyed the order and turned. Everyone else sat or stood motionless.

'I am troubled,' said Moluk, 'by the questions that are coming to me from this place. Let me answer them, fully and finally. Your Chairman, the other members of the Council and Dr Akiziwi are being held in restraint in the Library Annexe until after *Pegasus 5* has taken off. If any attempt is made to release them, the guards have orders to throw the deflation switches and kill everybody within this dome. Afterwards, using similar methods, the guards will control Port Imbrium until such time as they are able to follow us to Earth in a regular liner. These are my plans. If you accept them, no harm need come to anybody.'

The power emanating from the cold eyes in the naked mask-like head affected each person present. Steve fought against it. He said: 'Juan, why are you deserting us?'

The Spaniard put a gloved hand to his sweating forehead. 'Moluk is wise. I wish to inherit his wisdom.'

'Moluk is evil.' Steve's mind was being whipped by knotty thongs of persuasion. He defied the attack. 'Moluk has made you his prisoner as surely as Rod Bueno and the others are his prisoners.'

'Enough!' Moluk sensed a germ of uncertainty growing in Carranza and was quick to destroy it. 'The woman,' he said, 'is in the ship with Dominick and Ignatieff, who are checking over the systems before take-off. Time we went aboard.'

He reckoned that Steve and the others might talk and argue, but that on account of the danger to their friends they would do nothing actively to oppose him. In consequence he wasted none of his power in trying to bring them under mental subjection.

He and Carranza put on their helmets and left.

Steve was torn by frustration. Without the use of violence, which he realized would simply light a fuse for death, Moluk must have his way. He was kicking everybody aside, as he had kicked Kurt Lissner. Hate was irresistible.

For minutes after the departure of Moluk and Carranza, he stood by the coffee counter, with Norman, Kushi and Hans Lissner beside him and Tom Renoir in his chair in front.

Others in Recreation were staring in their direction, lost, looking for guidance. Because Steve had dared to question Moluk's will, they saw in him a possible leader. But Steve had no idea how to lead or to change the situation.

He saw the children filing in for their morning break from school, along with Janie and some of the other nurses coming off duty. Then, as he imagined Janie's fate if Moluk's philosophy were accepted, and the fate of children born and yet to be born, the ghost of a plan occurred to him.

Helmet in hand, Janie came across. He told her what had happened and what was about to happen, while Kurt and some of the other children stood around and listened.

'Oh, Steve, what can we do? For Renée, for Juan and Boris and Adam. Isn't there anything?'

Tersely, Norman butted in: 'We could do plenty. But the guards are in there, in the Library and in the Annexe. There are more outside. All conditioned to kill if we make one wrong move.'

Janie looked up at Steve and saw the pain in his eyes. Pain on her behalf. She put her arms about him and hid her face against the front of his vacuum suit. Clumsily he patted her shoulders, his affection and concern for her easing the pain.

And suddenly his expression altered. His eyes brightened. He caught her and held her at arm's length. 'Seems to me,' he said, smiling down at her, 'seems to me there *is* something I can do.'

It was almost 1150 hours.

Putting on his helmet, he went towards the air-lock.

The wings of *Pegasus 5* were spread, so that the down-thrust jets they contained would lift them high above the Moon's surface before the main atomic jets were brought into operation.

The time was 1155 hours.

Moluk and Adam Dominick were strapped into the white foam-rubber seats in front of the instrument panel. Juan Carranza and Boris Ignatieff, on the deck behind, had improvised safety belts out of nylon cord stretched between the seat supports and the ring-bolts in the door of the cargo bay aft. All wore suits and radio helmets.

Inside the cargo bay Renée Debussy was still without her

helmet. She was screaming and pounding on the door with ineffectual small fists.

An hour ago, when Boris had entered ADMIN to explain that the Chairman wanted her to make a brief journey to New York with a number of important papers for the Space Commission, she had been delighted, particularly as Boris, it seemed, was also going. Once inside the scout ship, however, she had been surprised by the absence not only of Rod Bueno but also of the papers she was supposed to carry. As time passed, she had become aware that Boris and Adam were acting strangely, with a cold and frightening indifference towards herself.

'When do I see the Chairman?' she had said, struggling to control her voice.

Boris had shrugged his shoulders. Adam – the charming, kind and always courteous Adam – had told her to shut up and stop worrying them.

Then fear had taken over as Moluk and Carranza joined the others and the air-lock was shut. Seeing Moluk's eyes on her, she had suddenly acquired an instinctive knowledge of what he intended to do.

When the air pressure had become constant, she had taken off her helmet and begun to scream at them, her blonde hair tumbling in confusion about her face.

'Shut her away,' had come the order from Moluk, and Boris had bundled her, screaming, into the cargo bay.

And now she continued to scream, terror constricting her throat and making her screams high-pitched. Nobody in the cabin heard them. Even if they had, they wouldn't have cared.

Adam had checked the instruments. The radar screen and radio transceiver were switched on. Reading figures from the chart clipped to the folding table on his left, he was programming the computer with details of his flight plan. The minute hand of the clock was jerking up to 1200 hours.

Issuing from Boris's helmet radio came a sudden exclamation. Quickly, Moluk, Adam and Carranza looked up and outwards through the wide port.

Adam said: 'What the hell?'

Moving on to the Landing Ground, ignoring the guards posted at the perimeter, were eight people in space-suits. Those inside *Pegasus 5* could see from their size that some were children and that one at any rate was a woman.

The stocky male figure heading the group raised a gloved hand. The others halted.

He came on alone and stood beneath the scout ship.

Into Steve's helmet, as he stood there directly under the nozzles of the lifting jets, there came a jumble of voices. He heard only one. It was Janie's.

'Steve, I'm coming, too.'

'No! Stay back!'

'I don't want to live if you are killed.'

'Stay back, Janie!'

But as he made a half turn he saw that she was already on her way. And that she wasn't alone. Behind her stumbled three children. He knew one was Kurt Lissner, the others were Kurt's friends, Nadia Corelli and her brother Alfredo.

To the small group standing fifty metres away he called out, desperately: 'Hans, Kushi, Norman! I told you I would do this alone. Stop them!'

But then his radio was silent. Janie was on his right, holding his right hand. Kurt was on his left, holding his left hand. The Corelli children were in front, pressing against his legs.

One broken voice came into his radio. 'Steve,' said Hans Lissner, 'I am proud of my son.'

In the cabin of *Pegasus 5*, confusion had come to Carranza, Boris and Adam. Only Moluk was calm.

He said: 'It is 1200 hours. Take off, Dominick.'

Adam heard the voice in his mind. Into his helmet radio he croaked a reply: 'We can't! The lifting jets will kill them!'

'What does it matter?'

'But Steve! Janie and the children –'

A blast of power seared in his brain. 'Take off!' commanded Moluk.

Adam's hand moved towards the jet switch.

'No!' exclaimed Boris. 'Let me speak to Steve!' Adam dropped his hand.

Boris took a shuddering breath. 'Steve,' he called, 'do you hear me?'

'I heard you, Boris.'

'Stand clear. Take Janie and the children!'

The answer came from Janie. 'We would rather die than live with Moluk.'

Juan Carranza got rid of his improvised harness. 'Steve, you are insane! Stand clear! We don't want to kill you!'

They were under attack from Moluk's thoughts – Adam, Boris, Carranza, the guards at the perimeter. But now something had happened to disturb the telepathic wave-length. Gradually a light was becoming stronger in the dark tunnel.

The guards were being summoned by their master to remove or kill the five people under the scout ship. But for the first time since Moluk had begun to exercise his spell, they were thinking for themselves. Listening to the gabbled talk in their helmet radios, they compared the selfishness of Moluk with the sacrifice that Steve, Janie and the children were prepared to make for others. They stood still and waited.

Carranza was remembering his life-boat comradeship with Steve. The memory became big and warm, like sunlight struggling through icy fog.

Adam imagined his hand on the switch and the chemical fire hurtling down. He saw bodies burnt and destroyed. He saw the eyes of his friends, Dr Hughie and Tom Renoir, agonized and reproachful. He was suddenly sure that he loved them all. He was suddenly sure that though Moluk was beside him, injecting hate, his hand would never touch the switch.

Boris, like Carranza, shrugged himself clear of the nylon cord. Even more quickly than the others, on account perhaps of his impulsive temperament, he was rejecting the cold cruelty of

Moluk. He and Steve were buddies in *Super Nova*. He had played childish games with Kurt Lissner and the Corelli kids. He had joked with Janie, who was Steve's girl. Now, with startling clarity, he saw his own girl Renée in Moluk's arms.

'Take off!' The order surged through their heads.

'No!' said Adam.

Moluk's brain worked swiftly to solve the problem. For once it failed to supply a logical answer. Something was resisting his will, a power he couldn't understand.

What he *could* understand, however, was the mechanical working of *Pegasus 5*. He leant forward to press the switch. But as he did so, in a moment of terror and exaltation, Adam bunched his gloved fists together and struck. Moluk fell sideways, kept in his seat only by his safety-harness.

Behind him Carranza rose. His arm crooked about the neck-piece of Moluk's helmet. He jerked the man's head back and in his radio heard a gasp of physical pain. Moluk's body went limp.

Boris opened the door of the cargo bay and caught Renée in his arms. He comforted her and told her to be quick and put on her helmet.

Adam unbuckled his harness.

Then the three men guided Renée to the air-lock and climbed out. With Steve and Janie and the children they stumbled across the Landing Ground, away from the ship.

At the precise moment that Moluk lost consciousness, the guards in the Library and in the Library Annexe emerged from a nightmare. They freed the Chairman and his colleagues, trying unsuccessfully to explain their conduct.

The nine men left Recreation together and joined their friends on the Landing Ground perimeter. With thankfulness Bueno saw that *Pegasus 5* was still there and that Renée Debussy, Adam, Boris and Carranza were amongst the group. From the chatter in his helmet he built up a picture of what had happened.

Then, as he endeavoured to impose order on excitement, tongues of flame shot down from the outspread wings of the scout ship.

He heard Carranza: 'I – I thought I had killed him!'

And Boris: 'He's taking off by himself. Heading for Earth –'

'No!' Adam's voice was tense. 'The computer is in control. Before I left the ship I negatived the tapes.'

Bueno put in, sharply: 'What does that mean?'

The answer came not from Adam but from the ship herself.

She rose against the indigo sky, high above the blue crescent of Earth on the horizon. Suddenly, from her fuselage, there erupted smoke. *Pegasus 5* hurtled sideways like a spatial crab, then plummeted down. In the horrifying silence of the Moon she crashed against the peak of Piazzi Smyth and in a slow-motion rhythm burst upwards and outwards into a million fragments.

Janie's gloved fingers were crushed in Steve's strong hand.

Share prices fell and arguments raged on Earth.

Bueno was blamed for mishandling the situation. The United Nations was blamed for not taking a stronger line with Moluk and the lunar colony. The Space Commission was blamed for losing the chance of exploring Saladin. With the benefit of hindsight, a great many people seemed to know what *ought* to have been done, especially the newspaper and television commentators.

But nobody thought of fighting about it, and despatches from Norman the News had a sobering effect.

A climate of tolerance began to spread. As Raymond Argonne remarked: 'In eighty years Saladin will again be close. Meanwhile, let us make the best of what knowledge we have.'

DIAGRAMS & TECHNICAL DATA

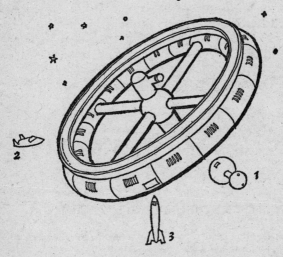

ALPHA MAIN SPACE STATION

Fully manned and orbiting the Earth at a height of approximately 2000 kilometres, it spins on its axis to simulate Earth gravity. Lying off are

1 a space liner, Archimedes type, and
2 a scout ship, Pegasus type.

A ferry rocket from Earth (3) is approaching the air-lock hatch.

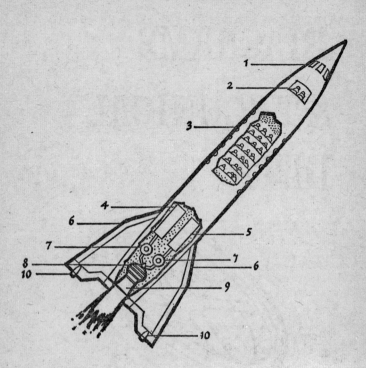

FERRY ROCKET (from Earth to Alpha Main)

1. Instrument chamber, instrument panel and observation ports
2. Pilot's compartment
3. Passenger cabin, with ports
4. Liquid oxygen tank (LOX)
5. Fuel

6. Wing-fins for glide back to Earth
7. Fuel pumps
8. Igniter
9. Thrust chamber
10. Auxiliary jets

SOURCE OF MAGNETISM IN ASTEROID SALADIN

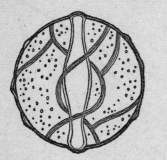

BATHOLITH
(cross-section)

SALADIN (cross-section)

Showing iron core, probably molten at centre but hard and in the
form of batholiths at poles, and the veins of ferrites composed
mainly of iron, cobalt, nickel, gadolinium and dysprosium.

Extract from article by Professor Parvo Salvonen published in
Monthly Scientific Journal for Schools (New York), October 2053:
'... Any current-bearing conductor (e.g. the ferrite veins in Saladin)
exerts a radial magnetic field, and the soft iron core simply
intensifies this magnetic field. At the atomic level this is explained
as follows. Every atom of every element consists of a hard nucleus,
positively charged, containing protons. This is surrounded by
magnetically-charged particles called electrons. These electrons are
the particles which carry electrical currents, and since moving
electrons exert a magnetic field, each atom exerts its own magnetic
field. Iron, cobalt and nickel and the rarer elements of gadolinium
and dysprosium and several alloys (e.g. alnico) possess the property
of aligning these minute magnetic fields so that they are additive.
The elements listed also *retain* this magnetism. In the case of
Saladin, the current source may be a reaction caused by extreme
heat at its core and comparative cold at its surface ...'

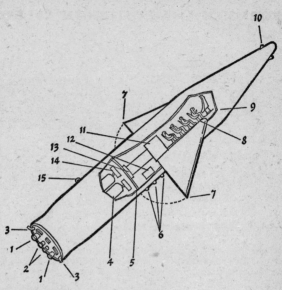

SUPER NOVA (modified 2052)

1. Main jets
2. Auxiliary jets
3. Rotatory jets
4. Atomic motors
5. Bulkhead
6. Horizontal lifting jets (there are four, one concealed by wing)
7. Retractable wings, for landing in atmospheric conditions (e.g. on Earth)
8. Seats for crew
9. Control panel
10. Nose landing wheel (retractable)
11. Equalizer
12. Airlock hatch
13. Toilet hatch
14. Water tanks
15. Eye-piece for towing

Underside of wing, showing landing wheels (retractable) and lifting and braking jets.

FORMS OF LIFE FOUND ON SALADIN

Amphipoda

Group of Crustacea,
including sandhoppers and
freshwater shrimps

Isoetes

Quillwort,
a sporophite plant

HEAD OF EASTER ISLAND STATUE

Similar to the statue found on Saladin, which Moluk so closely
resembled.

THE CAPSULE (OPEN) FOUND ON SALADIN

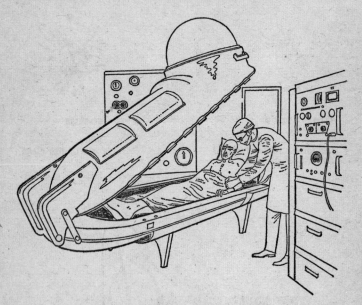

To a remarkable degree it resembles a modern hyperbaric chamber in which a patient is subjected to pure oxygen at twice normal atmospheric pressure to aid his recovery from acute myocardial infarction.